VICIOUS PRINCE

SPECIAL EDITION

STREET KINGS
BOOK TWO

SIENNA SNOW

To Natalie, ♡ Sienna Snow

STREET KINGS

BOOK 2

VICIOUS PRINCE

Copyright Page

Copyright © 2021 by Sienna Snow

Published by Sienna Snow

All rights reserved.

The scanning, uploading, and distribution of this book without permission is a theft of the author's intellectual property. If you would like to share this book with another person, please purchase an additional copy for each person you share it with. If you are reading this book and did not purchase it, or it was not purchased for your use only, then you should return it to the seller and purchase your own copy. If you would like permission to use material from the book (other than for review purposes), please email contact@siennasnow.com. Thank you for your support of the author's rights.

This book is a work of fiction. Names, characters, places, and incidents are the product of the author's imagination or are used fictitiously. Any resemblance to actual events, locales, or persons, living or dead, is coincidental.

www.siennasnow.com

ISBN - eBook - 978-1-948756-24-2

ISBN - Special Edition Print - 979-8-88535-009-9

DEDICATION

I dedicate this book to a group of women who believed in me, even when I couldn't believe in myself. Who made me laugh, listened to me cry, sent me dirty memes because everyone loves a hot guy, and most of all, encouraged me to write.

Patty, Shaila, Amalie, Reem, Meghan, Heather, and Colleen, we may not share blood, but you are my sisters. Thank you for having my back through everything. I adore each of you.

AUTHOR'S NOTE:

This is a dark romance and may contain subject matter that may be sensitive for some readers.
For details, please contact the author at contact@siennasnow.com.

1

JAYNA

"Why are you so interested in freelancing all of a sudden? Aren't your clubs keeping you busy?"

"Because I don't want my skills to get rusty," I said to my cousin Danika through my earbud as I leaned on the balcony of my penthouse in a high-rise overlooking Miami Beach.

Danika was what one would call an art appraiser-hacker extraordinaire. By day, she ran my former art gallery and appraised high-dollar artwork. By night—well, even during the day—corporations, government entities, and such hired her to harvest information for them. In addition to that, she was the Dark Web hacker the Little Rabbit known for using her skills for purposes that bordered on vigilante. In other words, she was an all-around badass.

I was her protégée. No, not really. Though she'd taught me

the ins and outs of the tech world to help with her caseload, hacking wasn't something I wanted to do as my career. I thrived in the world of clubs—dance and fight.

It wasn't refined. It wasn't classy. It wasn't sophisticated. It wasn't elitist. It wasn't a career a society princess liked I'd grown up to become would ever have chosen to pursue.

And of course, that's why I loved it.

I was a rebel, or so Danika liked to tell me. A person who marched to the beat of her own drum.

Well, why the fuck not?

I'd lost my way for a while, lived in a place where I thought I'd drown. Then I'd surfaced and decided I wasn't just going to survive, I would find a new purpose.

I'd moved to Miami a little over six months ago, built a life here, made friends, enjoyed time with my extended family, and started fresh.

But I missed the hustle and bustle of New York City. The slower pace of Florida took some time to get used to. And then there were still the memories that had followed me here. Though they didn't pain me as much as they used to.

"Do you ever sleep, Jay? I mean, don't you have like a hundred businesses to oversee?"

"Are you jealous that I can survive on a few hours and you need more?"

"I really hate you sometimes."

"No, you don't. So do you have anything for me or not?"

"It can't be about the money. You're fucking rich as hell. You're the only person I know who can start up a new venture and make a profit within months of opening."

I smiled at that remark. In my most recent endeavor, I'd

taken the idea of underground fight clubs and turned them into gritty-yet-upscale, exclusive, membership-only establishments known in New York City and Miami as the Ladai Room.

Ladai, in my family's native language of Gujarati, meant combat. I felt it was the perfect way to describe the place in one word.

It was almost unbelievable the success I'd garnered with the two clubs in less than six months. Currently, there was a year-long waitlist for membership at both locations. If the momentum lasted, I'd probably expand the clubs to various cities nationwide as I'd done with my nightclubs.

"You're right. It's not about the money." I closed my eyes. "You really want to know why?"

"I wouldn't have asked if I didn't want you to be honest."

"I miss you and New York. I like Miami, but I'm an NYC girl at heart."

"So, hacking makes you feel closer to me. That's so sweet," Danika gushed, making me shake my head and want to strangle her.

"Shut it, Dayal."

"I'm a King now. Remember?"

"Yes, we are the King sisters. Isn't that what the tabloids call us now?"

Danika was married to my brother-in-law, Nik, the eldest of the notorious King brothers of New York City. The public believed they were real estate developers who'd inherited the Midas touch from their adoptive father, Arin. But in fact, they ran an empire very few people even knew existed. They played brokers between polite society and the unsavory elements of the world. They dealt in favors, ones they collected on when it was to their advantage.

I'd married Kiran. The boy from the wrong side of the tracks. The boy with a dirty past. The boy who'd rescued me from a hell wrapped in privilege and society.

He was the enforcer of King Holdings, the collector, the protector, the weapon. Then one day, he was gone, leaving all of us, especially me, alone to pick up the pieces.

"Don't remind me. At least you're a thousand miles away from all the nonsense. Nik says if I ignore them, then they'll leave me alone. My job is about being sneaky. How the hell am I supposed to be sneaky with cameras in my face all the time?"

Danika liked to live under the radar and hated anyone noticing her. It was probably why she and Kiran had gotten along so well. They'd hide out in the shadows and throw the rest of us to the media. The problem was that both of them were insanely gorgeous people who'd always garnered attention.

"It comes with the territory. The Kings are big news."

"Easy for you to say now that you're in the Sunshine State."

"Do you think I don't have a million eyes on me here? I'm freaking surrounded by family. Mine and Kir's. It's like I can't turn around without someone wanting to know my business. Tell me again, why did I pick Miami?"

"Umm. Fresh start, year-round sunshine, the beach, hot guys, your mom. Did I mention, hot guys?"

"Don't let Nik hear you say that." I laughed. "Hey, when are you coming here so the family can harass your ass for a change?"

"Well—" She hummed. "I thought I could fly down for the

grand opening of your new club. Lilly said it was a sight to see when she was there to program all the lighting."

God, I couldn't wait until that bad boy officially opened. It was the crown jewel of all of my nightclubs. If there was one thing I knew inside and out, it was the nightlife business.

I also knew to hire the best when it came to designing them, and I'd brought on a friend of mine and Danika's new hire, Lilly, to develop all of the visual effects for the new club. Lilly was a tech genius, but unlike Danika, her specialty wasn't as much cyber as mechanical.

"Does that mean you're going to come early enough to get in a few sparring sessions before we hit the town?"

"Really? You're going to make me work out before we go clubbing?"

"You pay an exorbitant membership fee to the Ladai Room clubs, might as well check out the brand-new Miami location."

"I suppose," she grumbled. "I'm coming down for a vacation, not to have my butt handed to me."

"Think of it this way: I'll make sure the cocktails you consume equal the same number of calories you burn off."

"Whatever. Just for that, I should give you one of my dickwad clients to work on."

I felt a tingle of excitement. "Then you have something for me?"

"Yeah. Sending it over via the secure server."

I rubbed my hands together. "I'll get started right away."

"I swear, you're like a machine."

"You're one to talk. We're related, remember?"

"I'm going to crash. Jay, you need to sleep. It's fucking two in the morning."

"Yes, Mom, I promise I'll get some rest. Stop nagging me."

"You're such an asshole."

"Takes one to know one. Love you. Bye." I hung up the phone and set it on a nearby table.

Walking to the balcony corner, I set my elbow on the edge and stared out at the night sky overlooking the ocean. Even in the fall, the weather was hot and balmy. I lifted my face into the air as a warm breeze picked up.

In the distance, along the beach, my eyes focused on a figure I knew wasn't actually there. A man with eyes so observant they could see to the depths of my soul. A man who accepted my wildness and joined me, even when he was on the shyer side. A man with a will so strong that he would fight for me and everyone he loved until his dying breath.

Now, when I saw him, I viewed him as my guardian angel, not something to bring me pain. I'd loved him so hard that it had devastated me to know he'd left me alone.

I'd never love like that again. I'd never put all my hopes and dreams in one person again. I'd never let myself belong body, mind, and soul to any man again.

Only a fool would do that a second time. And Jayna Shah King was no damn fool.

A LITTLE AFTER NINE IN THE MORNING, JUST AS I WAS ABOUT TO review some proposal for an upcoming amateur fight at the Miami Ladai Room, Dillon Cortez, the location manager, walked into my office with an annoyed glare.

"Are you going to call him back or ignore the sixth message he's left for you this morning?"

"Ignore," I said as I looked up from my laptop at Dillon.

Dillon was Kir's younger cousin on his birth father's side and one of the few people I trusted with handling my business. As a former MMA champ, he knew the ins and outs of the fight world, the good, bad, and the ugly. But he also understood the concept I was trying to bring to the table with my clubs.

Dillon walked into my office and set a clipboard on top of my desk. "He's going to blow up your phone until you break down and return his call."

"I'm pretty resilient." I sighed and bit down the annoyance I felt every time my father, Ashok Enmesh Shah, decided I was supposed to jump at his command.

He'd disowned me as a daughter long ago and seemed to forget this fact whenever he needed to create an image of a united family front for his political career.

Papa was running to represent New York in the US Senate and needed me to show how much of a family man he was to the public.

Not happening. Ever.

Plus, I lived in Miami now. I had a new life here, had friends here. The last thing I wanted to do was go back to New York City. For him.

If I went back, it would be for Danika, Sam, Rey, or Nik. My real family, the Kings.

Besides, as a King, I had a reputation that could tarnish Papa's image.

Papa had taken Kir from me, and hell would freeze over before I did anything to make his life easier.

In fact, I planned to make his life as difficult as possible.

"There is no doubt about your strength," Dillon said. "You aren't the same woman you were two years ago. You're not even the same person you were six months ago. But Shah isn't going to stop until you respond to him."

"And that is why I have his number on ignore, and you get the calls, not me." I smiled.

Dillon narrowed his gaze and shook his head. "I really hate you sometimes."

"No, you don't."

If I gave Papa one inch, he'd jump at the chance to take more. He'd lied, stolen, and murdered to build his empire. He'd even filed a fake will giving him the inheritance my grandmother had wanted to go to her grandchildren.

Then he made one whopper of a mistake. He'd transferred ownership of his most lucrative subsidiary companies into my name when I was eighteen for tax purposes—a move I had no doubt he regretted over and over again throughout the years.

Now, he needed funding, and those companies could save his ass.

I may not want anything to do with Shah International, but it didn't mean I was going to hand over anything to a man who made nearly every day of my childhood a living hell.

No matter what Papa believed, I was no dummy. I knew how to play the game. The only way to keep him at bay was to hold him on a short leash and make sure he never got what he wanted.

Danika may have made peace with wanting revenge on Papa for taking her parents and her inheritance from her, but it didn't mean I had to feel the same way. Moving to Miami had given me a fresh start, but it had also shown me the wrongs of the past had long-lasting consequences.

Because of that bastard, I lost my husband, I lost my child, I lost my ability to have children. He deserved any hell I could send his way. And if he retaliated, I'd die laughing with the knowledge the man would never get his hands on the company or the money he needed to keep his precious Shah International afloat.

Pushing my dark thoughts back, I glanced at my watch and said, "Let's go over the roster for tonight. I'm having lunch with Luke, and I don't want to miss it."

"You've got a date with Lukesh Joshi, the hotel developer?"

"No, not a date. Luke's just an old friend. I told you we reconnected around the time I moved to Miami a few months back. He's in town from New York for the week and wanted to meet up."

"Are you sure there isn't something more going on between you two? You've seen a lot of him lately."

"Let me repeat. We are just friends. He gets me. We grew up together and have a shared history, most common among them being assholes for fathers who want to control our lives."

"I think he wants more."

"No. He doesn't. We have fun together. He makes me laugh. Besides, I have enough testosterone in my life with you guys around. No need to add more to the mix."

I pushed down the emotions that always came up when I thought of moving on from Kir. I'd tiptoed around the idea countless times over the last few months but never could let myself go through with it.

Something always held me back. Besides, what was the point? I would never risk my heart again.

"I hear you." Dillon smirked. "Some of us fighters are a handful. Let's go over the week's roster, and then I'm going to give you some ideas for an event I was hoping you'd approve."

2

KIRAN

"So, you're actually going to do it?" my brother Nik asked me over the phone as I worked my left hand through the daily muscle training it needed in order to keep its mobility.

Finally, after over a two-and-a-half-year battle, I'd gained back nearly all the physical strength I'd had before the wreck that had destroyed my life.

A wreck orchestrated by my father-in-law, Ashok Shah, and his partner, so I would no longer be a problem for their plans when it came to my wife and the power she had as the heir to a billion-dollar property development empire.

"Yes. I've waited long enough."

"It's about fucking time."

I set my weight down and walked to the back of my gym, picking up a bottle of water and then returning to the bench.

Uncapping the lid, I chugged down the water and then stared at the picture of my beautiful wife on the wall.

It was a picture I'd taken of her walking along Miami Beach. Her thick, shoulder-length hair blew all around her from the breeze, and she had her face turned up to the sun. Breathtaking was the only word to describe her.

"She's probably going to shoot me. Hell, I know there's at least a ninety-nine percent chance she'll pull a gun on me and then tell me she's going to finish what she had to live for the last few years."

When it came to tempers, Jayna's was like a volcano. She fought as hard as she loved. Maybe it was the fact she hadn't had a voice in the home she'd grown up in, and with me she'd felt safe, or maybe it was just the woman she'd become. All I knew was that it turned me on like nothing else, even to my detriment on many occasions.

God, the number of times we'd ended up fucking like rabbits to burn off the energy of an argument before we settled down enough to have a rational conversation.

If that happened, I'd be a lucky man. But that hope was a very remote, if an unlikely possibility. I'd fucked up royally, and I'd have to make amends to my princess.

"It's the least you'd deserve."

"True. I won't deny it."

"What are you going to tell her?"

"The truth."

"What exactly is the truth? You can't give her any bullshit. Telling her about the contracts isn't going to cut it. She'll see right through it."

Yes, there was a price on my head. There always was a price

on my head, and Jayna understood the world she'd entered when she'd become my woman. Whether a business rival put a contract on me, or in this case, her father and his associates, the precautions were all the same.

Though in this instance, she was acceptable collateral damage, and no way in hell was I okay with that.

I glanced at my reflection in the mirror along a wall of the home gym. One half of my body was nothing like it had been. I was no longer the pretty boy with the baby face my brothers loved to rag on me about until I punched them.

Now I was a reconstructed puzzle of skin, pins, and bone.

A work of modern medicine.

I touched the not-quite-normal left ear reconstructed from pieces of rib, cartilage, and skin. Then, I traced along the jagged scars that ran from my temple, over my eye, my cheek, and down my jaw. The physical changes only gave a glimpse of what I'd become after the accident.

I'd lived in my head for so long.

In the chaos of the crash and the aftermath. In the pain.

God, there had been so much pain. I'd been on the verge of madness. First, just surviving and then trying to learn basic things like eating without looking like a fucking toddler. After that had come the rehab when I'd begged for my brothers just to kill me and finish the job the wreck hadn't done. But the hardest part had been the mental toll. I'd become a shell of the man I'd been.

I'd lost my way.

When an enforcer had no strength, he had nothing. He was worthless. To his brothers and especially his wife. Locking myself up with my painkillers had been the only solution. Or so

I'd convinced myself. I'd turned into a raging addict and the worst version of myself.

"I'm going to tell her that I was fucked up in the head after the accident, that I was worthless to her and everyone, that I believed it was better she thought I was dead than for her to live with what I had become, that it was my shortcoming, not hers, for the decisions I made. That I was a coward and afraid she wouldn't be able to look at the monster I'd become."

"It's good to hear you sounding like the old Kir again. No bullshit. Owns his part and is willing to accept the consequences."

"Yeah, I'm finally doing what everyone wanted me to do. I'm getting my head out of my ass."

"She's going to give you hell."

"I expect nothing less."

"When are you going to do it?"

"Tonight. Jayna is heading to her mom's after work, according to the itinerary she gave her security. I thought I'd go over there. That way, if she freaks out, her mom can handle it."

"Monica is going to kick your ass too."

My mother-in-law was one of the kindest people I knew, and she'd endured hell with her ex-husband. Now that she'd created a new life, she'd found her voice and had no problem using it, just like her daughter.

"I know."

"And what will you do if Jayna can't accept your apology?"

"I'll work my ass off to win her back."

"Does this also mean you're coming back and finally doing your job like you're supposed to?"

"I have been doing my job, asshole."

"Yeah, behind a desk. Like a pussy. We need you out and about. Fewer idiots to deal with if they know you'll come to collect. You're the boogeyman of the King brothers. They don't call you the vicious prince for nothing."

He knew damn well I wasn't keeping my ass chained to a fucking desk. But since I wasn't working on the frontlines, I was a slacker.

It had been that way since we'd run the streets of our shit neighborhood in New York City, scamming and fleecing dumb tourists who wanted an authentic Big Apple experience. By the time, Nik and I turned nine, we ran with the local crew. And even at that age, we were expected to pull our weight.

"I hear you. Let me first survive the wrath of my wife, and then we'll deal with the issue of my coming back from the dead."

"We already knew you were coming back. All you need to do is walk out into the sunshine, Shadowman."

Nik made it sound so easy. And maybe it would be.

"Just like that? No explanations, nothing."

"Just like that. We're Kings. We make our own rules. That was Arin's motto, or did you forget?"

"No, I didn't forget."

To say my adoptive father was unconventional was an understatement. From our first encounter when Nik, Rey, Sam, and I tried to steal his wallet, Arin never followed the expected path. Instead of killing us as most men in his position would have done, he'd taken four street kids in and given us a new direction, a new life, showing us a way to use our natural talents and skills to our advantage.

He wasn't the type of father to hug or use affectionate

words. And truth be told, none of us would have appreciated it. He was tough, giving us no bullshit, but always showed up when we fucked up. There was never any judgment in his eyes.

Nik was a lot like him. Solid, broke for no one, and created his own rulebook.

"It's going to fuck with a lot of people's heads."

"Do you give a shit?"

"The only person that matters to me is Jayna."

"Then go handle your business. But remember what I told you long ago about women."

"What's that?"

"Hell hath no fury like a woman scorned. You better be ready. Jayna is going to eat you alive."

I closed my eyes and prayed to God she left me in one piece.

3

Jayna

"Think about it, Jayna. You know we would be good together."

I almost groaned inside and had visions of punching Dillon for putting it out into the universe that Luke wanted more from me.

I would probably go through with it when I met up with Dillon for our training session tomorrow morning.

My lunch with Luke was everything it usually was—fun, laid-back, easy, until this very moment.

And I blamed it all on Dillon.

Yes, a punch to the nose was definitely in store for him.

I glanced out the restaurant window at the groups of beachgoers on South Beach before returning my gaze to Luke's handsome face.

I studied him for a moment.

He had the polished good looks of a Bollywood movie star, and he definitely knew how to dress, no matter the occasion. He was smart with multiple degrees and a bank account that rivaled mine. Plus, we'd been friends since we were children. He was the ideal Indian boy to match my pedigree in the uber-affluent society I'd grown up in. The only difference we had was that he still lived in that world, whereas I'd run as far as possible from the pomp and circumstance.

I opened my mouth to respond, but he stopped me by lifting a hand and saying, "Just hear me out."

I sighed. "Go ahead."

"I understand why it would never have worked when we were kids. Our parents tried to push us together, and we wanted different things."

I almost smirked at that. Not parents, fathers.

It had been some arrangement between Arun Joshi and Papa for the "sake" of their business relationship. They'd set up some arcane contract stating I'd marry Luke after I graduated college, and in exchange, their two companies would merge.

Papa viewed his family as a commodity and moved us around like chess pieces. And if we dared to disobey, we suffered at the end of Papa's fist or with a kick.

Even the fear of his discipline hadn't stopped me from rebelling. If there was one thing I was good at as a child, it was making Papa see red. If he said jump, I'd sit. If he told me to dress conservatively, I'd come out in something revealing. In a home where I'd had no power over my own life, this was a way to push back.

Then when I'd turned eighteen, I'd packed my bags and left.

Thank God for the limited trust fund my maternal grandparents left me, or I wouldn't have had any place to go since no one from the affluent Indian community I'd lived near would have helped me. Papa had thought if I got desperate enough, I'd come crawling back home and fall in line.

Truth be told, even without the trust fund, I'd have found a way to leave. I'd made a promise to myself that I would never endure the life my mother lived and that one day I'd help her get out.

"Before you go further, answer this question. Did you know about the agreement between Papa and your dad when we were younger?"

Luke clenched his jaw. "I learned about it after you left home. I'm sorry. You have to know I never agreed to any of it. I was with Seema then."

Luke's eyes grew sad for a moment before he hid the shadows of the past. I reached out and set a hand over his. He was one of the few people who'd experienced the type of loss I had. Seema was the love of his life and had died of a heart attack due to an undiagnosed heart condition a month before their wedding.

"I'm sorry. I shouldn't have brought it up."

"No. Our past is what has us here today. Isn't it time for both of us to move on?"

I shifted to pull away, but Luke took my hand in his.

It had been two and a half years since any man had held my hand with any intimacy, and this felt wrong on a level I couldn't explain.

I swallowed, schooling away the turmoil inside me, and said, "Right now, I can't offer you anything more than friendship."

"Jayna, what better foundation for a potential relationship than friendship?"

Maybe I shouldn't have gotten together with him so much over the last few weeks. At first, it was to reconnect with a familiar face from NYC. I'd invited him to join group gatherings and introduced him to many of my Miami friends. Then, I realized I enjoyed hanging out with Luke. He made me laugh like I hadn't in so long. But there hadn't been any romantic spark.

Maybe it was my internal resistance from what Papa had done to force me to marry Luke or…

Who was I kidding? There was no denying the reason why I couldn't see myself with anyone, Luke or not.

One man haunted my mind, my heart, my dreams, my soul, and ruined me for anyone else.

Kiran King.

I glanced down at the wedding bands that hadn't left my finger in over two years and then looked up at Luke. "I wasn't trying to lead you on."

He squeezed my other hand. "I know you're not. Will you answer this question?"

I nodded.

"Why did you leave everything in New York?"

"To start over," I answered without hesitation.

"Doesn't that mean leaving the past there? Including—" he paused, "—Kir?"

Something roiled in my stomach, knowing what he said was

partially true. I'd moved to get over the past and to let it stop haunting me.

Time and distance from New York had made the ache ease. But there was no getting over Kir.

One thing I could say for sure was that I'd discovered a strength in myself that hadn't existed in so long, and I'd found a purpose.

Hell, Dillon loved to tell me I was a badass boss, kicking ass in a business dominated by men.

Maybe Luke was right. I should give him a chance, even if it was short-term. I was allowed a little fun.

I knew there was no epic love for me ever again. That was a road a girl only went down once in a lifetime.

Luke and I were friends. He knew my past, and I knew his. And, it wasn't fair for me to condemn him for something our fathers tried to force upon us.

I glanced down at my wedding rings again, knowing it was time to take them off. I'd give them to Mummy today when I went to her house. She'd keep them for me.

I could do this.

Baby steps.

Taking a deep breath, I said, "Okay, I'll go out with you. But I won't make any promises."

Surprise flashed across his handsome face, and then his lips curved up in a big smile.

"Before you get excited, I just want to make sure you understand that I'm a King and what comes with it."

He frowned, releasing my hand. "What does that mean?"

I leaned back in my chair. "We have a reputation, Luke.

People may not like that you're associating with me on a personal level."

I wasn't ever going to shy away from who or what I was for anyone. When I'd met Kir, I'd entered a world that dealt in things that many wouldn't consider legitimate. But then again, Papa had created an empire pretending he was above reproach and had swindled people right and left.

"Your husband had a reputation. Your brothers-in-law have reputations. You don't. You're a King by marriage."

"No, Luke, I'm a King. I was never a Shah, no matter what Papa may believe. Kir and I were together for years before we married, and that whole time, I was the one who ran his businesses outside of King Holdings."

"What are you trying to say?"

"I want to make sure you understand dating me means the Kings come with the package. They are forever my family."

He studied me, a slight crease forming between his brows before it smoothed away.

After a few moments, he nodded. "Understood. Family doesn't always mean blood. First, I win you over, then them."

I smiled. "Let's see if we can make it beyond friends. As I said, I'm not making any promises."

"Challenge accepted." Luke lifted his wineglass in my direction, and for the first time in a long time, I felt lighter. "How about we start our date now?"

"I wish I could. I still have a full day of work ahead of me, and then I promised my mom that I'd spend the evening helping her pack for her trip to the BVI." I picked up my glass of water and sipped. "How about tomorrow night?"

"It's a date." He smiled at me again. "An official one."

A LITTLE BEFORE SIX IN THE EVENING, I TOOK THE EXIT RAMP OFF Interstate 95 and headed in the direction that would lead me toward the upscale neighborhood where my mother lived. After my lunch with Luke, I'd met with the staffing specialist for my nightclub and then spent most of the rest of my day in meetings going over the possible expansion of the Ladai Room clubs.

I'd had to make it clear to a few overzealous and pushy developers that I was not now nor ever interested in their help in managing my venture.

Condescending fuckers.

People assumed because I was a woman who'd grown up in a supposed ivory tower that I had no idea how the fight world worked. What they seemed to forget was that I'd learned everything I knew from the best.

The King brothers.

Specifically, from Kiran.

At a young age, Kir had lost his parents in a tragic accident and fallen through the cracks of the foster care system, ending up on the streets and running with a gang. A gang led by his brother, Nik. The gang had become his family, teaching him how to survive and use his fists.

By the time he was a teen, he'd started organizing underground matches as a way to make extra money and never stopped. For him, it was a way to bond with those around him.

When we'd first met, Kir had done everything to show me he wasn't the man for me. He would play up the dirty side of his life and get into the cage more often than necessary, thinking it would send me screaming. What he hadn't realized was that seeing the raw strength in him turned me on more than the intended repulsion he expected. The pampered princess box he kept trying to shove me into never seemed to fit, and then, the day I least expected it, he claimed me as his.

Eventually, I was the one scoping out the underground locations and setting up the matches. Kir only posed as the face since it made it easier to gain credibility and a higher purse.

Yep, it was misogynistic as hell, but that was how I had to play the game. And it was easier to manipulate the assholes into doing what I wanted than to always get in their face and fight with them.

By the time Kir and I'd married, everyone in our inner circle knew and accepted I was the one who ran the operation.

Kir would jokingly say I was the brains, and he was the brawn. We were the perfect partnership. He never questioned my business sense. In fact, he seemed relieved to have no part in it. In contrast, I loved to have my hands in everything.

I smiled.

Wow. I'd actually thought of Kir without any pangs of pain.

Maybe the universe and Dillon weren't fucking with me after all.

It was time to move on.

Even Dillon's mother, Kir's *Tia* Martha, told me to dip my toes in the dating pond when she'd stopped by the club this afternoon. She'd gone as far as to insist I let her set me up with a "nice" boy she knew.

I should find comfort knowing I had the support of Kir's extended family. They knew I'd loved Kir with all my heart and would always cherish our time together.

When I'd first met Kir, and we'd become serious, he'd flown

me down to Miami to meet his family. A family he'd only learned about after his adoption. They were a true cultural blend of Puerto Ricans, Indian-Guyanese, and Americans. Most of the older generation lived within miles of each other, and they knew everyone's business.

Kir's parents hadn't had a star-crossed love story like Kir and I'd had. They'd both been immigrants, his father from Puerto Rico, his mother from Guyana. They'd met at work, fallen in love, married, and then had Kir. The only tragedy was that shortly after moving to New York for work, they'd both died in a bus accident, sending Kir into the foster care system. A system he'd run from and eventually forced him into the world that brought him to the doorstep of his adoptive father, Arin King.

Kir and Luke were polar opposites. That was probably a good thing. And since Luke lived in New York and only came down to Miami every few weeks or so, I knew it could be a fun fling, no commitments or long-term anything. One all-consuming love was good enough for this lifetime.

Horns blared around me as a truck ran a red, and I slammed on the brakes, causing my tires to screech.

"Fuck. Damn Miami drivers," I shouted, smacking my hand against the steering wheel, and then laughed.

Who was I kidding?

New York City drivers were the worst. The number of times I'd nearly gotten run over by cabbies were too many to count.

My phone rang to the distinct tone of Queen B's song "Run the World," telling me it was Danika.

She probably wanted an update on the project. I'd blown through the assignment she'd given me and then worked on some personal business dealings. The skills I learned under Danika's tutelage came in handy on a regular basis, specifically when applied to keeping certain aspects of my businesses hidden from prying eyes.

By working in a business dominated by men, they always wanted to know what I was doing and poked their noses in places where they didn't belong. Keeping my information protected under layers upon layers of what Danika and I like to call cyber red tape kept the assholes of the world at bay.

Pressing a button on the console, I answered, "Hey, lady, how's it going? Did you see I finished the project? Got something else for me? If you do, I'll overnight you a case of Firewater."

Danika was obsessed with whiskey, and I had exclusive distribution rights for one of her favorite brands, Firewater. It was an elderflower-infused spirit created by a friend of mine, that went for nearly a thousand dollars an ounce depending on the bottling.

"Jay, stop talking and listen. I need you to get off the road now." The panic in Danika's voice had my heartbeat accelerating.

The last time I'd received a call like this, she told me Kir had been in an accident.

"What's going on?"

"Find somewhere safe until I can send security."

I looked around me to see if I could spot my personal detail. They were always with me.

Since the moment I'd gotten together with Kir, I'd had personal security. Kir's role in King Holdings caused people to fear him or want to get to him before he could get to them. The best way to get his attention was through me, and therefore I had a detail with me at all times.

Initially, it annoyed me, but most of the time, I barely noticed them. They left me alone, and we were friendly to the point one could be friends with people who liked to be invisible.

Where the fuck were they? They should have tagged me by now. They were supposed to be the best.

"Dani, I need more information. Besides, this is Miami. I can't just pull over anywhere."

"Dammit, Jay, do you have to fucking question every damn thing? I came across some chatter about a double hit out on you."

My skin prickled.

Would Papa put a hit out on his own daughter?

Of course, he would. He'd done it before. He'd rather send others to do his dirty work instead of getting his own hands dirty.

"Who ordered it?"

"We can't be positive on any source. I'm trying to work it out. All I know is that there are two orders."

As the congestion around me cleared and I started to move, I noticed a car that seemed familiar.

A green Hummer.

Yes, Hummers were all over the place in Miami, but a green one, no way. On South Beach, that colored car looked artsy and unique. Out here near Indian Creek Village, it stood out.

"Dani—" my voice quivered, "—I think someone's following me."

"Shit. Why the hell did you lose your security?"

I clenched my jaw. "It was a game. We do it all the time. They usually tag me within a minute or two."

"This was the wrong day to fuck around, Jay." She growled in frustration. "I'm going to see if any of our men are in the area. Otherwise, I'm going to call Van."

I looked in my rearview and saw the Hummer getting closer as it weaved between cars. "Yes, I think Van might be the best option. She has people everywhere."

Van was Devani Patel, a friend of ours who worked for an underground spy agency known as Solon. If there was anyone who could help me at the last second, it was her. She had people tucked away all over the world and could mobilize them within seconds.

"Is there any way you can get back on the main highway?" I could hear Danika typing on her keyboard.

I looked at all the side streets leading back to the interstate.

"I could, but it might take a minute. It's rush hour, so the traffic is insane." I made a right, thinking to loop around the block.

"What are you doing? Why'd you turn?"

"This street is the fastest way to get back on the high—"

At that moment, the Hummer slammed into the back of my Mercedes, propelling me into the van in front of me. My whole body jerked forward as my airbags deployed.

Stars burst behind my eyes as pain shot throughout my body.

"Jay!" I could hear Danika screaming from the speakers, but I couldn't respond.

My mind was in a daze.

The windows of my car shattered.

A few seconds later, someone reached in, opening the door. "We have her."

"Hurry. There are too many cameras around here."

The next thing I knew, two sets of hands were dragging me out of the car. That was when my brain finally functioned enough to struggle. I shifted one of my arms enough to grab the throat of the man carrying the top half of my body and squeezed, digging my nails deep before I folded my legs in and then jerked them out. Both men lost their hold on me, and I fell to the ground, jarring my back against the asphalt.

"Motherfucker!" one of the guys shouted. "That fucking hurt. Get the bitch."

I crouched, ready to kick out if anyone came toward me. I would never let anyone take me again. The day I died, it would be on my terms.

Through the haze of a headache brewing, I noticed another group of men approach with guns drawn.

What was going on?

Fuck, there was no way I could get anything from inside the car.

Where the hell was I supposed to go? I had no phone, no wallet.

Shit.

"She's ours," a man with a heavy New Jersey accent said.

"The fuck she is." One of the guys who'd pulled me from the car stepped between me and the man with the gun.

Knowing I wouldn't have long before their attention shifted to me, I crawled my way backward against my car. My hands scraped against broken glass, but I held in the scream.

God, that hurt.

I knew Papa was behind this.

If this was how he wanted to fuck with me, I'd make sure he paid. I fucking knew how to protect myself now. I wasn't that weak girl anymore. I'd lived a lifetime in the last few years.

I shifted to move and heard a gunshot, making me flinch and crouch down further.

Breathing through the pain and letting my anger guide me, I slowly crawled under my car. I couldn't run without drawing their attention, and I'd rather have them fight it out than get hit in the crossfire.

Just as I positioned myself as far away from the confrontation happening, I heard a voice that shouldn't exist.

"Princesa, come with me. I'll keep you safe."

Nausea filled my stomach.

What the fuck?

He couldn't keep me safe. He was dead. He left me when I needed him most.

It was my mind playing tricks on me. It had to be. I couldn't go down that road again.

I'd worked too damn hard for this shit to happen. Maybe the hit to my head was harder than I thought. I had a killer headache. That had to be it.

Breathe, Jayna. Breathe, Jayna. You are not losing your mind.

I rolled into a fetal position and closed my eyes, hearing another gunshot in the distance and shouts of people looking for me.

"Baby, I have to get you out of here. We don't have much time."

I covered my ears. This was not happening. I refused to let it happen.

I was stronger than this. I had survived so much.

"Dammit, over two years and you're as stubborn as ever. I didn't want to do this, but you leave me no choice."

A cloth-covered hand clamped over my mouth and the world disappeared.

4

KIRAN

I ANSWERED MY PHONE AS I WALKED INTO MY BATHROOM, TWO hours after Jayna's abduction. "I have her."

Nik sighed in relief and then asked, "How is she?"

"Fine," I responded as I glanced over to the bed where Jayna lay motionless.

Even with scrapes and cuts on her skin and a dark bruise covering the side of her face, she was breathtaking. Over two years of separation hadn't changed the natural beauty of the only woman who'd ever owned my heart.

All I wanted to do was crawl in bed next to her and pull her close.

When Nik had sent word about the double hit out on Jayna, I'd just reached Miami and had nearly gone out of my mind trying to get to her location. I'd made it in time to see her kick the face of one of her assailants and fall to the ground. Just when I was about to intervene, another group arrived, giving me the perfect opportunity to grab Jayna. I hated having to knock her out, but the only other choice was to scare her out of her mind and draw attention to us.

"Is she hurt?"

"Not too bad. Bruises, mainly. And few cuts on her hands. She'll be sore, but there isn't anything to worry about."

"Are you sure?"

I clenched my jaw. "Yes, asshole. I would know if my wife was hurt or not. I've had more medical training than you have."

When we'd arrived at our property off the Keys, she'd floated in and out of consciousness. Barely making any sounds as I'd removed her clothes, checked her body for injuries, and cleaned up the grime covering her skin. After slipping one of my T-shirts over her head, I'd laid her on the bed and let her sleep.

"She doesn't know it's you. Does she?"

"No. But then again, she hasn't really woken up enough to understand what's happened. I think she's just sleeping. She seems utterly exhausted."

"Danika says she barely sleeps more than a few hours at a time. The only time she's ever known her to sleep through the night was—"

"With me." I finished his sentence as a wave of guilt hit me. "I know."

I knew Jayna's history. The abuse she'd lived through and the nightmares that haunted her dreams. I'd promised to keep her safe and for a short time, I had.

I had a lot to make up for.

"Any word on who ordered the hits on Jayna?"

"According to Rey, he's still tracking one of the sources, but the other is your idiot cousin, Hector."

"That makes no sense. Why the fuck would Hector target Jayna? She's no threat to him."

"Hell if I know. Rey's digging, and I'm sure Danika is doing her own search. All we know is that he made an unexpected visit to *Tia* Martha today."

"That's too damn coincidental."

"My sentiments exactly."

Hector was the illegitimate son of my Uncle Luis. Part of a family I hadn't known existed outside of my parents for most of my life. It wasn't until after Arin had adopted me and connected me to *Tia* Martha that I'd learned my history.

When my father, Antoni, left Puerto Rico with his sisters, he'd left behind a father, three brothers, and a very lucrative arms and drug syndicate. Through time and the nature of their business, the only living family members remaining to take over the Silva Familia were Hector and me. And out of the two of us, my grandfather, Victor Silva, had chosen me as his heir.

I never planned to live anywhere but in mainland USA. My life was in New York City, and no amount of status or money would change it. It wasn't about the crux of the Silva business. As a King, I never walked the straight and narrow, and we worked daily with people who had their hands in everything, legal and illegal. It was about the family I had with Arin and my adoptive brothers, Nik, Rey, and Sam. That was a bond nothing could break.

I'd signed over my claim and inheritance, even going as far as to name Hector rightful head of the family. However, Victor had rejected my stance. In his eyes, I was the legitimate heir carrying the Silva name, and therefore owned everything.

It hadn't mattered that Victor had raised Hector in the business from the moment he'd gasped his first breath or that Hector was as ruthless as Victor could ever have dreamed of being.

Fucking traditionalist.

Then, when Victor passed around the time Jayna and I married, I'd sent word to Hector that I wanted no part of the business and to have at it. I'd assumed it was the end of the issue.

But it seemed I was wrong.

"What did he want from *Tia* Martha?"

"She said he asked her about some of her cargo contacts and making introductions. He wasn't happy when she told him to get lost. And before you say anything, we've added extra people on her."

"Fucker is setting up to expand stateside."

"Looks that way."

"Where is he now?"

"Our eyes say he was waiting for a package at a private airfield. I can only assume it was Jay. When it didn't arrive, he took a plane back to San Juan. It landed an hour ago."

"What does he get by going after Jayna?"

"It makes me wonder if her moving to Miami has him suspicious that you're alive."

"It's been over two years. Why would he wait until now to question it? Besides, her mother lives in Miami. It's not a farfetched idea for Jayna to move near her."

"She hired your cousins to manage her businesses. She even

sent two of them up our way to oversee the NYC location. You have to admit, the kind of loyalty she garners from your family is pretty intense. She continued what you used to do."

Jayna always drew people to her. She had a way about her that made everyone feel important. And she loved with a passion. Once you were in her inner circle, you were hers forever.

"Fuck." I glanced over to the bed and muttered, "Jay, what have you been doing to get on Hector's radar?"

I braced my palm on the marble vanity counter.

"That's a question you're going to have to get answered. Jayna has as many secrets as my wife does. Even more so since she came back from Greece."

About a year ago, Greek billionaire Sylvia Thanos had decided Jayna needed a vacation and whisked her away to her island off the coast of Greece. Whatever Sylvia had done to Jayna, it had lit a fire in her. She decided to leave New York and went full force into expanding her businesses with a single-minded focus.

"The answers will have to wait until after she tries to gut me."

"We all have to pay the piper at one point or another. You're just lucky he held out as long as he did."

"I hear you."

"By the way, your contact said the scene was a mess and clearing it was a pain in the ass."

"They'll get over it," I muttered. "I've helped them out enough times."

"Are you going to confess those activities to your wife as well?"

"Yes. It's time to put all the cards on the table and see where the chips land."

"I suggest you get some sleep while my wife and Rey do their hacker work. You're going to need all the rest you can get to deal with the wrath of Jayna."

"Speaking of your wife, tell Dani that I'm sorry for putting her in the middle of this."

"You tell her the next time you see her. I'm sure when Jayna finds out Danika knew and kept your secret, she'll have to deal with her own shit."

"My sins are catching up with me."

"We're all sinners. It's how we repent that matters. Get some rest. I'll report back in the morning." Nik hung up.

Setting my phone on the counter, I leaned forward and studied my face. I'd come a long way from the man who couldn't look at himself without cringing.

Men like me and my brothers, those forged by the streets, weren't allowed to break. We pushed through every hurdle, ignored the pain, and pretended we had no weaknesses.

I knew I'd let them down. Hell, I'd let my wife down.

My brothers had forgiven me, and now I could only hope Jayna would as well.

I was the enforcer, the protector, the one sent in to make sure everyone followed the rules.

It was time to do my job. Jayna was in the path of enemies seen and unseen. I'd be dammed if I'd let anything happen to her again. I may not have been able to protect her after my wreck, but I sure as hell could now.

Scrubbing a hand over my face, I pulled off my shirt and shucked my pants.

I might as well take a shower and get some rest before the sleeping tigress woke and ate me for breakfast.

5

KIRAN

"Yes. Right there." I moaned and shifted, wanting more of the soothing, heavenly salve easing the pain constantly running up and down my skin.

Soft and delicate, light and gentle.

Dear God. It was almost as if I could feel the press of Jayna's luscious lips against my neck.

The likelihood of this being anything more than a dream was impossible.

Too many nights, I'd opened my eyes and found myself alone, aching, wishing to turn back time.

Full hips and thighs straddled my waist, and I couldn't help but groan and buck up into the incredible sensation of my woman's pussy rubbing against my boxer-covered, straining cock.

This had to be my mind's sick version of torture.

"Kir," Jayna whimpered as she rubbed up and down my length. "Why won't you touch me? I need you to touch me. Don't let me wake up without you touching me."

Immediately, I froze. My brain fired to life as I opened my eyes to find Jayna staring down at me through desire-clouded hazel irises.

How many mornings had I woken in the past to this gorgeous woman exactly like this? To her hands exploring me and then riding me until neither of us could think of anything but the need to come?

"Princesa." I couldn't hide the panic in my sleep-roughened voice.

One of her delicate fingers glided down the center of my face, over my lips, and along the column of my neck.

"You're so handsome, Kir. You were never too pretty, as you liked to say. You were perfect for me."

She definitely wasn't awake if she saw me as perfect.

"I need you to lie down next to me." I glanced at the clock to see it was past two in the morning. We'd both slept for nearly five hours.

She pressed a finger to my lips and then leaned down until we were nose to nose. "I want to fuck, Kir. I ache so much. All day, sometimes. Then I dream of you, only to wake up every time it's about to get good."

I clenched my hands by my sides, refusing to grip her hips and do what both of us wanted.

"This isn't a dream. I need you to look at me."

"I am."

"What do you see?"

"The ghost who I can't let go. My lover. My man. My husband. The man who promised to stay with me until I took my last breath. The reason why I refuse to fall in love again."

Direct fucking blow to the heart.

"Jayna." I lifted up and she immediately pushed me down with two hands flat to my chest.

"If you're going to leave me like every other time, I want to explore you." She nuzzled my cheek. "It's my right. I'm your wife."

"That's not a good idea, baby."

"Of course it is. Besides, you're the one who says morning sex is the best way to start the day."

I was going to hell. Fucking going to hell.

I closed my eyes, unable to relax and unable to resist the need for her touch.

This was a disaster waiting to happen. When Jayna learned the truth, there was a chance she wouldn't be able to look at me.

Her graceful fingers and nails grazed over my neck and throat, sending goosebumps over my skin.

The press of her lips to the center of my chest had my cock jumping and bumping up against her slick, rocking cunt.

This was an erotic torment I knew I'd die from.

She moved lower, her lips and hands trailing a path down my abdomen.

Fuck.

I had to stop her before it went too far.

She pushed me slightly to the side, tracing one of my tattoos, one I'd had extended after my accident.

"This is new." Her tone and breath changed as she explored the ink covering the scars on my side and back.

The sensation of having anyone touch my skin was almost too much. The fact it was Jayna exploring, seeing the damage the wreck had caused hidden under the ink was both a blessing and a curse.

What would happen once she woke and realized I was a liar, the villain of the fairytale, and not the hero as she believed? Would she listen to me and forgive me? Or gut me as I expected?

She pushed me again onto my back and then straddled my hips, her eyes scanning all over me, almost frantic until they landed on my wedding band—a wildness filling her gaze.

"You never took it off."

"Only when they made me."

God, I was talking to her as if she could understand me.

What the hell was I doing? I had to stop this.

But the sick bastard part of me couldn't. I needed this little time before she realized this wasn't her imagination.

She set my hand on her breast, but I let it slide to the bed, making her frown.

"Do you love me, Kir?" she asked in that voice she'd use whenever she was determined to get what she wanted.

"More than anything on Earth."

"Then touch me." She pulled off the T-shirt I'd changed her into, exposing her incredible breasts that made my mouth water with the desire to taste them.

"I can't. Not until we talk. Not until you've forgiven me."

She grabbed my hands and set them over her bare breasts, using my palms to squeeze the mounds.

This was torture, not the dream I thought I was having.

"I don't want to talk. I want to touch. I want to fuck."

I pulled my hands free and tried to dislodge Jayna, but she'd clamped down with her knees and thighs against mine.

When the hell had she gotten so strong? It had to be all those hours she spent training at the club.

"It's not that simple, Jayna."

"Yes, it is. Do you want me?"

"Of course, I fucking want you. I would love nothing more than to get lost in your body. This isn't the right time." I pressed my palms to my face.

This was my penance for the last few years. It had to be.

"Fine. If you aren't going to participate, I'll take care of it myself."

She reached down between our bodies and gripped the ridge of my cock through my boxers. Throwing back my head, I bucked up into her hold. I couldn't help but revel in the incredible sensation. Nearly three fucking years without her hands on me.

"Please, Jayna. If we do this, you're going to hate me."

Her gaze met mine as she pushed down my underwear, just enough to free my cock, and positioned me at her soaked entrance.

"Oh no, Kir. I do hate you. As much as I love you," she said as she slid down a fraction. "You fucking bastard."

I froze, realizing she was completely awake and pissed to holy hell.

"Now fuck me, or I'll kill you using that knife I'm sure you have hidden in that top drawer."

I stared into eyes filled with hurt, anger, and betrayal, knowing I was about to enter a storm.

"Do it," she ordered as her hair tumbled around her shoulders.

I should stop this. Do the right thing. Try to reason with her.

But damn, I needed her so fucking much. So instead of pulling her off me, I gripped her round ass and brought her down hard, burying myself to the hilt.

"Fuck, Jayna."

The feel of her cunt was better than ever. The heat of her, the way her muscles molded against my cock, the scent of her. There was nothing like how she smelled, not her perfume, but her natural, earthy, pure essence.

"Don't move," Jayna gasped, closing her eyes. "I…need to get used to this again. God, I missed you inside me."

Her beautiful face was a play of pleasure and need.

"Baby, I have to move. It's been so long. I won't last."

She opened her lids and her lips curved up, not in amusement but calculation. "Whose fault was that?"

She rolled her hips and I all but saw stars.

I held her down with my palms while lifting up onto my elbows. "If I come, you won't get to come."

"Says you," she challenged. "I've spent years taking care of my own needs. You aren't necessary for that particular service."

Hell, the fuck no. That was not how this thing between us worked.

I flipped her onto her back, keeping my cock buried deep inside her and then pinning her arms above her head. "Let's get this clear. You come if I allow it. Every one of your orgasms belongs to me."

Fire burned in her hazel eyes. "You don't deserve them."

"I don't, but they're mine." I shifted my hips until I pulled out to the tip and then slammed in, making both of us groan. "From this point on, I own this body. Even if I don't deserve it, it's mine."

I thrust into her again and again.

"You don't own me. No man will ever own me again. Especially not you."

"If I didn't own you, then why didn't you take a lover? Why didn't you find another man?"

"I fucking hate you." She bit my shoulder so hard that I knew she'd drawn blood, then all of a sudden, she threw her head back and screamed, "Don't stop. Don't stop. I'll kick your ass if you stop. And believe me. I know exactly how to kick your ass now."

Her pussy quivered and flooded my cock with arousal.

Maneuvering her wrists into one hand, I slid the other between our bodies and to her swollen clit. Slowly, I strummed the delicate bundle of nerves in the rhythm I knew would send her over the edge into oblivion.

"Kir," she cried out as she clamped down on me, arching up and squeezing her eyes tight.

The force of her release pulled the strings of my control to the point of snapping.

Freeing Jayna's arms, I caged her head and reared up, setting a hard and fast pace. Every dormant nerve in my body awakened and wanted all the sensations denied to them for so long.

When Jayna wrapped her legs and arms around me, it was a slight reprieve from the tempest I'd only just entered.

This was my woman—the princess from the ivory tower who'd left everything for the street rat.

My heart.

My balls began to draw up, and I knew I couldn't hold out much longer. But I had no choice but to wait. The change in Jayna's breath told me she was climbing again.

"Do you want to come again?"

"Yes," she gritted out as if she was pissed to admit it.

"How do you want me to do it?"

She closed her eyes, refusing to look at me. "You know how. I need it."

"It's a sign of submission."

"I know."

"Look at me. You want this. Own it."

The anger and desire were back in her hazel gaze, something I'd rather see than sadness and resignation.

Shifting my weight onto one arm, I slid my palm over her throat, collaring it with my fingers and then squeezing, not hard enough to hurt her but giving her the pressure she desired with the combination of my thrusts to send her over. Instantly her body responded and her core contracted around my length.

I wasn't going to lie and say it didn't do something to me to know she craved this from me. That she still trusted me enough to want this from me.

"That's it, let go." I continued to pump in and out of her, pushing her closer and closer to her peak.

Sweat dripped from my forehead, and I blew out a breath, holding in the growing need to come.

"Oh God. Yes. Oh yes." Her back bowed and she clenched down on me so tight that I saw stars and went over with her. Both of us lost in the mindlessness of release.

6

JAYNA

How could he do this to me?

I tried to catch my breath, warring with feelings of wanting to cry, beat the shit out of the man lying half on me, and fuck him again.

He'd all but destroyed me when he'd died, and now... Now what?

I couldn't even wrap my mind around what was happening.

One second, I was in the middle of an abduction, then I was dreaming about my dead husband who wasn't. And on top of everything, my body had woken from its hibernation and now was demanding satisfaction.

How could I want to fuck again when his cock had barely pulled free of my body?

Maybe I was still dreaming. Please let this be just a bad dream. He wouldn't do this to me.

"We need to talk," Kir said without lifting his head from my shoulder.

No luck. Not a dream.

I stared at the ceiling, studying the multicolored glass that made up the structure. The design looked so familiar, similar to something I'd sketched with an architect long ago.

All of a sudden, a lump formed in my throat. "Where are we?"

"The Keys."

No. He wouldn't.

"Where?"

He lifted onto his forearms to stare down at me. "You know where."

I bit my lip, feeling the tears I refused to shed well behind my eyes.

Kir and I'd bought a small private island off the Keys to build a vacation home. We'd started construction when Kir had his accident. I'd assumed everything had stopped after I'd ordered Nik to sell the property. I couldn't have imagined coming to a place with so many memories.

"Have you been here the whole time?"

"Since a little bit before you moved to Miami," he answered and then added, "I was in New York before that."

A rage like I'd never felt before began to bubble up inside me. "You bastard. How could you?"

I shoved Kir to the side with all the force I could will into my arms and scrambled off the bed.

This was too much. I had to get away from him. I needed space. I couldn't think.

I looked around, trying to figure out where to go and knowing I was stuck. I was on a goddammed fucking island.

We'd picked this spot for its remoteness. And I had no doubt Kir rigged this place with state-of-the-art surveillance and security. No one could arrive or leave without Kir's approval.

In the past, Kir's ability to keep me safe, keep the world away was something I needed, craved. Now all I wanted was to run, run far away from this. Whatever *this* was.

I could feel the panic bubbling up inside me.

Too much was happening.

I grabbed and wrapped a sheet around me and then moved to the opposite side of the room, needing as much distance between Kir and me as possible.

That was when I felt the warm, wet slide of Kir's cum on the insides of my thighs, and my arousal immediately ignited.

Oh God. I didn't need this now, on top of everything else.

I swallowed down the war of emotions readying to overwhelm me. I had to get myself under control.

"Princesa." He stepped toward me, and I raised my hand, staying him while using my other to hold up the sheet.

"Don't you dare call me that. You don't have the right."

"We're married. You gave me the right when you became mine."

"No, I'm a widow." Tears clouded my vision and my body shook. "Kiran Antoni King died in an accident two years, eight months, two weeks, and five days ago. The man I loved would never have let me live knowing he was alive. He would have trusted me. He would have fought tooth and nail to stand by my side."

"I was wrong." He took another step toward me as I retreated. "I made so many mistakes."

"Mistakes. Is that what you're calling it?"

"There are things you don't know."

"Obviously." I clutched the fabric tighter around my body before gathering enough sense to secure the sheet with a knot between my breasts. "Start talking."

I kept my distance from him, walking along the wall of windows overlooking the water until I reached his bedside table.

Kir shook his head and moved toward me.

"Stay there. I don't want you anywhere near me right now. Not until I get answers." He froze, and I pulled open the top drawer, expecting a knife like he'd kept in our place in New York but found a pistol instead.

Grabbing the gun, I pointed it at him and reflexively Kir lifted his hands in the air.

He couldn't come near me. My emotions were all over the place. I wanted to shoot him and fuck him all at the same time.

"I'm not going to hurt you." He circled me.

"Stay right there, Kir. And stop looking at me like that."

"How am I looking at you?"

"As if you could disarm me in a few moves. I know you're calculating the steps. Don't even think about it."

Kir had trained all his life in some form of combat or another. Even when he ran the streets of his old neighborhood in New York City, he was known as the kid who knew the maneuvers to take down any opponent.

He stopped advancing, knowing I'd caught on to what he was doing, and then backed away. "Would you shoot me, Princesa?"

The pain of him calling me by that pet name was too much.

"I'm not your princess. I'll never be anyone's princess ever again."

Princesses depended on others too much. They let others dictate their futures. I'd done that too long. First with my father, then even if I'd chosen it, with Kir. Never again would I let myself fall into that.

"And for the record, I will shoot you. Then everything I've lived for the last few years won't be a lie."

His lips turned up slightly at the corners, making me want to pull the trigger.

"Jayna, baby. Listen to me."

"Don't you dare *Jayna baby* me anything."

"The accident wasn't my choice."

"Yes, I know. It was my father who set it up."

"No, I need to tell you all the details. There are things you don't know. I wasn't in my right mind. The reasons why—"

"I know all the details," I cut him off. I couldn't linger on those memories again. "I saw the footage of that night. Danika showed it to me before she destroyed it."

A few months ago, my father had tried to use the footage of the accident as a way to frame Kir's brother Nik for murder. The video showed Nik moving Kir's body. A body I assumed was dead. Danika had called in favors and used her hacker skills to make anything implicating Nik in Kir's wreck disappear.

"I didn't want you to see it."

I cocked my head to the side. "That wasn't your choice. But I guess you think it's your right to make decisions for me. Well, let me make this clear to you, I had a right to know the truth of whether my husband was dead or alive. I had a right to be there by his side while he recovered. I had the right to make the call if I could handle something or not. And most definitely, you should have been by my side this whole time. I needed you." I shouted the last part as I remembered the stabbing and the loss of our child.

"I'm sorry. I know I failed you." The anguish on his face was too much for me to handle when my emotions were so raw.

I wanted to turn away, but I'd lived a lifetime since he left, and I could handle anything. "I would have stood by you."

"Dammit, it wasn't about you standing by me. It was about what I'd become standing by you."

I stalked to him, anger burning under my skin, but before I realized that he was moving, he'd pulled the gun from my fingers and tossed it on the bed.

He held my hands in his, and we stared at each other.

Breathing heavily, I said through gritted teeth, "I'm looking at you. Did you think your scars would revolt me? Is that what you think of me? That I'm that fucking shallow?"

He closed his eyes as if I couldn't understand what he was saying. "You deserved better than me, always have. This was something your father and I agreed on."

I jerked my hands free, using the very moves he'd taught me, and shoved his chest with enough force to push him back a few steps. "Don't you dare. Don't you dare give me that copout. I had a right to be there for you. I had a right to know you were alive."

"Jayna, I wasn't the man you knew before the accident. I was barely hanging on."

"I needed you. Do you know what it would have meant just to know you were there?" All of a sudden, it hit me. "You couldn't have made the initial call on this, could you? Nik, Sam, and Rey had to have helped you."

A complete sense of betrayal settled on my shoulders.

Kings stood together. We were a team.

They were my brothers, and they hid this from me. Intentionally kept me from my husband. So many people had kept Kir from me. People who claimed to love me.

Oh God. That meant even Danika was part of this.

"Did Dani know?"

"She found out by accident. She stabbed me when it happened." He rubbed his arm. "She's loyal to you. More than you believe right now."

"Yet she still kept your secret," I said.

"Don't be upset with them. They did what they thought was best."

"Tell me."

"I was in a medical coma for a little over three weeks, then in the hospital for another eight. After that, countless surgeries and physical therapy. Then the real pain started. I had to get my life together looking like this." He pointed to his face and body. "I was in a bad place. You would have left me if you'd seen the monster I'd become."

How could he believe I'd see him as a monster?

"Our love wasn't about the surface, Kir."

"I wasn't a good person. I'd become an addict. I had rage. The kind of rage I'd never want you to see. At the time, I'd rather have you believe I was dead than put you through any more trauma."

I knew he meant the stabbing and miscarriage. That was a place I couldn't visit right now. A place I'd worked too hard to lock away.

"I want to know all of it."

"It's going to take some time to get through everything."

I clenched my jaw. "Why don't you start with the physical since that seems to be one of the many things you thought I wouldn't be able to handle."

He released a sigh as if resigned to the inevitable. "Follow me."

I studied his offered hand. His wedding band glinted from the reflection of the lights in the room, making me remember when I'd asked if anyone had found the ring and the disappointment I'd felt when no one had.

Now I knew why.

Instead of sliding my hand over his, I walked past him into the giant master bathroom.

I paused for a second, letting the impact of the space hit me. It was everything I'd envisioned it would be, with floor-to-ceiling walls of glass giving views of the water, a giant walk-in shower with multiple showerheads, and an oversized tub big enough to fit both me and Kir's six-foot-two fighter's body.

He'd finished our dream home without me.

Pushing down the rage, I stopped in front of the double sink vanity.

Kir motioned to shift me to face the mirror. Instead, I stepped out of his reach. "No. You don't get to touch me."

We stared into each other's eyes for what seemed like hours.

There were so many emotions running between us—pain, hurt, anger, need, lust, and as always, love.

"It may be easier if you looked in the mirror."

"For who? You or me?" I couldn't hide my bitterness.

Kir released a deep breath and nodded.

"This—" he traced along the side of his face, over the edge of his eye to his reconstructed ear and down his jaw, "—was after four surgeries over a year-and-a-half period."

Without thinking, I reached up, but he set my hands on the counter, shaking his head.

He turned to the left, pointing to a spot near his ribs. "This is where a piece of metal punctured my lung and came out the other side."

I couldn't help the grimace.

"All of this." He gestured to the puckered skin hidden under the tattoos on his arm, back, and side. "Is the result of months of skin grafts."

"How long was the total recovery?"

His brown eyes locked with mine. "Physically, I'd say about two years. Mentally, it's a work in progress. It took a while to get out of that dark place."

"What got you out of that dark place?"

"Rehab, a therapist who wouldn't take any bullshit, and the knowledge you were moving on if I didn't get it together."

But I hadn't. Well, not until today. The Universe was definitely fucking with me.

"Were you ever going to tell me?"

He gave a halfhearted laugh. "You're not going to believe it, but I was actually on my way to your mom's house to see you tonight."

"Why Mummy's?"

"I wanted to do it somewhere you felt safe. Somewhere you had support. Just in case you freaked out, your mom would be there to calm you down. She can handle anything."

"You mean somewhere you were protected from me killing you."

"That too." Kir's lips tugged up.

Mummy loved Kir with all her heart. He was her son, and he could never do wrong in her eyes. Knowing her, she'd forgive Kir immediately for putting us through this.

Too bad I wasn't the same.

Logically I could understand the dark place.

I'd fucking lived there too.

I could even understand having to fight through addiction.

But he'd taken my choices away from me. Hell, my family had taken my choices away from me. And that was something I wouldn't get over easily.

"Am I supposed to accept this and welcome you back into my life?" I asked, feeling the well of emotions bubbling up again.

"I don't have any expectations."

"Isn't that big of you?" I narrowed my gaze and clenched my fist, ignoring the slight sting in my palm from the scrapes I'd gotten during the abduction. "I'm so glad you aren't making decisions for me anymore."

There was a roaring in my ears from all the anger brewing inside me. I wanted to hurt Kir as much as I hurt right now.

And I wanted to fuck him too.

What the hell was wrong with me?

The scars, the change in him, didn't revolt me. It was still him. My damn idiot husband who'd just broken my heart as much as he'd done when I thought he'd died.

"Why are you looking at me like that?"

I cocked my head to the side. "Like what?"

"Like you want to whale on me and fuck me at the same time."

"What if I want to do both? Would you let me? I think I'm due." I moved toward him.

"You want me to let you punch me?"

"Would you take it if I said yes?"

"Probably. Does this mean you're going to put Dillon's training to use?"

"It's tempting. You'd deserve it. But that's not what I want to do."

"What do you want?"

I lifted a brow. "You know what I want."

"That's a bad idea." He shifted backward.

Moving closer, I said, "Because of you, I went without for nearly three years. I'm due. And I plan to collect. Preferably while I draw blood."

Kir retreated farther. "You're no way in the condition for that kind of play."

"And what condition would that be?" I moved forward as he continued going back.

"Jayna."

I almost laughed, seeing the wariness in his eyes.

He could overpower me without a thought. That was the plan. He owed me.

"This is only going to complicate an already volatile

situation." He licked his lips and set his feet in a stance I knew well.

"Are you telling me no? From where I'm standing, your cock is saying yes."

"My cock is never going to say no to fucking you."

"You owe me."

"I'll owe you until my dying breath. We need to talk first."

"Oh, we're going to talk. We have years of things to discuss. I'm going to make you pay in spades for not trusting me, for making decisions for me. Right now, you need to take care of my body."

"Sex is only a temporary fix."

"So be it. You made promises to my heart and body. You broke them."

"I'm not fucking you, Jayna. Not until we settle things."

"Are you refusing me? I can still find someone else to satisfy me, and then I wouldn't need you."

Kir narrowed his gaze.

I brushed up against his chest, scoring my nails over his shoulders and then letting one of my fingers press into the spot where I'd bitten him. "I am within my rights. I am a widow."

Kir clenched his jaw and gripped my hips, his boxer-covered erection hard against my stomach.

Rising up on tiptoes, I gazed into his dark eyes and said, "I can fuck another man. I can fuck a dozen men. And you have no say in the matter."

"Let's get this straight. You are not a widow." He growled, hurling me up against the wall and pinning my wrists above my head. "I am your husband. I'm very much alive and I will break the neck of anyone who dares touch what is mine."

Something inside me had to have known Kir was alive. It was the only explanation for my resistance to ever starting anything with anyone or the constant ghosts I kept seeing.

No. There was no fucking ghost. Kir was the fucking ghost, haunting me.

"Then are you going to fuck me while I'm fully awake?"

"And what about regrets?" His resistance completely shattered as he rubbed his stubble-covered jaw against my neck.

I arched against him. "We have plenty of regrets between us. This isn't going to be one."

"I hope you're right because you're about to get exactly what you asked for." Without a word, he lifted me and carried me to the large counter between the sinks.

He set me on the counter, staring into my eyes a second before he fisted my hair and jerked my head back. My heartbeat accelerated, and a flood of desire pooled between my legs as a brown-eyed beast I hadn't seen in so long crept out of the shadows.

His teeth bit my neck with the force and the pressure that had me gasping and goosebumps prickling down my spine.

"Kir," I moaned, holding onto his forearms.

He lifted his head, shifting back to untie the sheet, and then picked me up and turned me as if I weighed nothing, positioning my knees on the stone vanity.

He set a hand to the hollow of my back. "You're a fucking goddess."

I stared at my reflection, naked, breasts large, nipples aroused and puckered, knees splayed open, pussy glistening and completely visible, and face flushed with desire.

How long had it been since I felt like this?

Too long. Too fucking long. And it was all Kir's fault.

"Now it's time to make a discussed fantasy a reality."

God, I'd forgotten. We'd talked about this when we'd designed the house.

He stepped closer, bracing my back against the front of his body, his crisp chest hair a heady sensation I hadn't felt in so long. Goosebumps pricked down my spine and over my skin, and the urge to press my knees together drove me for a moment.

God, it had been so long. This driving need.

Fuck. He hadn't even touched me. Not the way I needed him to, and I was going out of my mind.

It was the sexual deprivation I'd put myself through. That's what it had to be.

"Look at me, Princesa."

I frowned then noticed a slight smirk on his lips and knew he'd said it to annoy me, in the exact way he'd done when we'd first met a decade earlier. When I was the untouchable high society princess from the mansion, and he was the street fighter with a shady background and no pedigree.

"Don't call me that. You don't have the right. I didn't give you permission."

He cupped my throat, holding it in that way that had me wanting to give him anything and everything. My core contracted and my breaths grew shallow.

"You wanted this," he said, biting my earlobe. "I may be scarred and have a whole shit-ton of things to make up for, but one thing will never change. When it comes to this body—" his other hand pinched one of my nipples, causing me to arch forward, "—I command every inch of it."

"Kir," I couldn't help but whimper as I clutched at his arms. He shifted my face. "Watch my hand."

I opened the eyes that I hadn't realized I'd closed and watched him as he teased the puckered tip of my breast with light tugs and then slid his palm lower.

Something passed in his eyes as he traced over the jagged lines on my stomach from the stabbing, and then it disappeared. I was thankful he hadn't gone there. I wasn't sure I'd ever be able to talk about it. It was better to leave it in the box I'd locked those memories in.

He gathered my hair, shifting it to one shoulder, and licked from my ear to my shoulder. I arched into the tingle his tongue sent throughout my body.

God, that mouth of his.

His fingers delved lower between my spread thighs. He circled my clit, drawing my arousal around it, round and round.

"Oh fuck." My thighs quivered.

"Yes. We're going to fuck but not yet. I've never known a woman to have such a beautiful pussy." He continued to tease me. "Do you have any idea how many nights I jacked off to the memory of it?"

"That was your fault. You could have had the real thing." I dug my nails into his arms and smiled when he hissed.

He plunged a finger deep inside my channel, making me gasp. "That's true. I have years to make up for."

Immediately my core quivered around him, and then the second digit joined the first, followed by a third as his thumb worked my clit.

I bit my lip and moaned, loving the pleasure-pain. It had been so long, and I needed this so much.

Why did I need this so much?

"I love seeing you ride my fingers. God, Jayna. I could come from just looking at you like this."

I watched us as I rocked to the motion of his hand.

Fuck, this was everything and more than I imagined when we'd talked about being in this room. My wetness glistened down my thighs and over his fingers as his other hand held me at the throat. Both of us desperate for the other.

Hot, dirty, raw.

"Kir. I'm close. Harder. Faster. Dammit."

"No, you're not."

I clenched my teeth. "You wouldn't."

He smirked and nipped my earlobe with his teeth. "Wouldn't I?"

He teased and tormented me, plunging in and out of my pussy, bringing me to the point of going over and then easing up on the movement so my release hung just out of grasp.

"Kir. You bastard," I cried out the fourth time he brought me to the cusp and denied me.

"Are you ready to beg yet?"

"I won't beg." I blew off the hair that had fallen into my face and then glared at him in the mirror as I saw the smugness on his gorgeous face.

He curved his fingers deep inside me, increasing the stretch inside my pussy to an almost deliciously painful level, and then pressed against the sensitive spot only he'd ever found.

"Kir, dammit, let me come," I screamed as the wicked torment of his hand became too much.

"Is that the best you can do?"

I could only growl and score my fingernails down his arms.

"You're such a stubborn woman." He pulled out completely, angling me forward slightly.

"Don't stop now, damn you." I sobbed and then I moaned as his cock rimmed my entrance.

"Do you want this?"

"Yes. Damn you."

"Look at me."

I shifted my head to lean back, but he grabbed my jaw and positioned it so I looked at the mirror. The scene before me was beyond erotic and everything I'd dreamed of for over two years. My husband behind me. His cock poised at my pussy, ready to pleasure me. Him controlling all of my desire.

He released my neck. "Hold on to the counter. I don't have much control left."

I followed his directions as he held my thighs open and pushed in.

"Fuck, finally." I gasped, falling forward onto my forearms.

Kir pummeled my pussy, hard and fast. Soon the only sounds in the room were moans, gasps, and sex.

I braced one palm against the mirror and held Kir's gaze in the reflection. The raw hunger I saw staring at me ratcheted up my need to a level I hadn't felt in years.

With only this man.

I loved him and hated him for it.

All of a sudden, some semblance of reality hit me.

What the hell was I doing? I needed to get answers, not fuck him. Not let my physical need overwhelm my thoughts.

"You wanted this," he said between thrusts. "Don't you dare check out."

"I'm not checking out," I countered, meeting the movement of his hips with mine.

"I know you. I know every fucking thing about you, Princesa."

"My body," I gasped as my pussy contracted around his cock. "Maybe."

"There is no maybe about that one." He shifted his hips, rocking against the sensitive ball of nerves deep in my core, and everything inside me tightened as my orgasm overtook me.

I threw back my head, clenching my eyes shut and crying out, "Don't stop. Oh God. Don't stop."

He continued to ride me, pounding so hard that he pushed me from one wave into the next.

When he finally called out his own release, I dropped my forehead onto the counter and whispered, "You may still know my body, but you have no idea who I am, Kir. The woman you abandoned doesn't exist anymore. She had to grow up and learn how to survive on her own."

7

KIRAN

"God, I shouldn't have waited so long," I muttered to myself as I walked to the white marble half wall that marked the edge of my patio and gazed out at the water.

The sun was just over the horizon, giving the picture-postcard view of the Keys the travel photographers tried to capture. From this vantage point, only a few other islands were near us and all owned by people who treasured their privacy.

I'd found this spot knowing it would be an escape from the life Jayna and I had in New York. A place to take a break from the hustle and bustle of our work. Then there was the stress of her father trying to find one way or another to break us up.

When we'd gotten together, Ashok Shah had viewed me as a stain on his affluent family's linen. A half-breed Indian, as he'd called me, wasn't good enough for his daughter. Shah had plans for Jayna that did not include me. If only he'd known that I wasn't the one who had chased after his precious daughter.

She'd come to one of my underground fights, decided I was her man, and stuck around until I'd caught on that I couldn't live without her.

From the beginning, she'd gotten under my skin, but I'd let her believe I wasn't interested. She was the girl who had men falling at her feet, and it seemed as if she enjoyed the hunt as much as I liked having this beautiful woman work to get my attention.

It wasn't until the day I saw the vulnerable woman under the facade of the princess playing on the wrong side of the tracks that I'd fallen. She'd brought out a protectiveness in me that I'd never felt for anyone else in my life. And from that moment, there wasn't anything I wouldn't do for her.

I glanced behind me, toward the house and up to the tinted glass walls of the bedroom where I'd left Jayna two hours earlier.

After our bathroom escapade, we'd showered and ended up fucking again. We couldn't get enough of each other, no matter how messed up our situation was.

Even now, I was half-hard, just thinking about her sleeping naked in our bed.

I was dealing with a different woman now. Well, maybe not completely different, but she'd changed.

The woman you abandoned doesn't exist anymore.

Jayna's words echoed in my mind as guilt and shame filled my chest.

I turned back to the ocean and closed my eyes.

I had abandoned her. I'd failed her, as a husband, as her best friend, as her protector.

Lifting my face up to the sun, I let the ocean breeze wash over me.

I would fix this.

There was no other choice. But first, I had to confront Jayna about the information Rey had discovered this morning.

Damn woman had no idea what she had done. How the hell she'd kept this a secret from everyone, including Danika, was beyond me. Then again, there was a chance Danika knew and had kept it from all of us.

I only hoped the plan Rey suggested would work.

And for the plan to work, I needed Jayna's cooperation. That also meant we had to have an actual conversation without jumping each other.

I cupped the back of my neck. I was swimming up a shit creek.

"Kir, where are you?"

Turning, I looked in Jayna's direction as she came outside and paused.

Fuck me.

She had on one of my white tanks and a pair of my black training shorts, both too big and jerry-rigged to fit her somehow. The outlines of her dark nipples were visible through the thin material of the top, telling me she hadn't found the underwear I had drying in the laundry room.

Her hazel eyes heated as she took me in, wearing only my lounge pants, and my cock jumped in response.

It was as if she couldn't see my scars or the changes in my face or body.

She licked her lips, and her gaze shifted to my growing erection.

At least we had one thing going for us. Our marriage was on life support, but our physical need for each other was as strong as ever.

"No," she muttered to herself and shook her head as if trying to push the lust away.

If only it were that easy. I hadn't been able to calm my body since I'd woken with Jayna gyrating on top of me hours earlier. Coming three times inside her hadn't done anything to alleviate the clenching need.

She stalked toward me. "Give me a phone."

"No." I leaned against the half wall that made up the end of the porch. "We need to clear up some things first."

There was no point in trying to hide the tent my cock was making in my pants.

"The hell with that." She cocked a hand on her hip. "I need to call my mom. She was expecting me at her place."

"Danika called her. She asked her to cancel her trip and come to New York."

"And where did she tell her that I went?"

"She said a property you had your eye on had come up for sale, and you and Sam were flying out to see it. Your car is currently back in driving condition and parked in a private hangar at the airport."

She clenched her jaw and poked a finger against my chest.

"Mummy isn't stupid. She would have seen through that line

of bullshit, even if you had my car planted to corroborate the story."

"You're right. She didn't believe any of it. But she understood the meaning behind Dani's call and followed directions. Ever since she left your father and the chaos of my accident, Nik had procedures implemented for her to follow if we needed her placed under protection."

My mother-in-law, Monica Shah, had lived a life full of fear and pain under her ex-husband's rule. When she'd left him, I'd made sure she always had a way to escape to safety with specific code words and messages that would let us know she was in trouble or allow us to convey a situation was dangerous.

"And the scene? Everything happened during rush hour."

Instead of responding, I glanced down at the well-manicured nail pressing into my bare chest and then up into those blazing eyes made golden by the sunlight.

She had to know there would be no evidence of the abduction anywhere. She was well versed in how the Kings operated. We kept our business out of the public eye and used every means necessary to ensure it happened. Hell, back in the day, she'd have assisted me in the cleanup of incidences like hers.

"You didn't."

"Didn't what?"

"What favor did you call in?"

I almost smiled. If she only knew.

"Does it make a difference? It's done."

Her eyes narrowed. "Who called in the favor, the Kings or Danika? I need to know who I'm indebted to."

"Neither—they were mine. That means you're indebted to me."

She clenched her jaw. "What the hell does that mean?"

"Within moments of us clearing the scene, my team swept the area and made all traces of the abduction scenario disappear. This includes all physical evidence, camera feeds, and GPS tracking. You're familiar with how it works."

"That isn't what I was talking about, and you know it."

"I'll give you the details about everything once we discuss what happened yesterday."

"You want to discuss what happened yesterday?" She pushed my chest. "The asshole I married who let me believe he was dead for nearly three fucking years kidnapped me. That's what happened yesterday. Now give me a damn phone. I want to get off this fucking island."

The spark of temper flaring to life in Jayna's eyes told me she was on the verge of going nuclear.

"Jay, we aren't leaving here until we have all the details on why you were a target yesterday," I said in my calmest voice, knowing the only way to deal with Jayna's temper was to stay the fuck calm.

"In other words, I'm a prisoner here?"

"This is your home. I wouldn't call it a prison," I responded.

"A cage is a cage, no matter how pretty it is." She stepped back. "Let me make this clear. I will never again live my life in fear."

"Fear is the last thing I want you to feel. I want to protect you."

"I don't need you to protect me. I can do it myself."

"Dammit, Jayna. I will not put you in harm's way again."

"I'm not the girl you left behind, Kir." She lifted her chin. "I don't need to stand behind the vicious prince of the King brothers anymore. I've managed on my own for the last few years. I have no problems continuing to do it."

Turning her back to me, she moved toward the house.

She was still stubborn as hell.

I pushed off the half wall and followed behind her, and as her steps grew faster, so did mine. A second before I grabbed her arm, she abruptly stopped, dropped to the ground while pivoting to the side, and kicked my feet out from under me. My back hit the grass so fast I could barely comprehend what happened. Jayna pressed a foot to my chest as she leaned over me. Her beautiful face flushed, and her breath came out in hard pants.

"Don't ever think I'm weak," she gritted out. "I don't need you to protect me. That girl died with you. And I won't be her ever again."

"I don't think you're weak." I flipped her so I had her pinned under me. "Having me near doesn't make you weak."

She bucked, shoving me off in a move I'd only seen fighters use in the cage. Damn. She'd gotten strong. I weighed a good eighty pounds more than her.

Crouching on the ground, she watched me as if I was about to pounce on her.

"Depending on you or anyone isn't something I will ever do again. I'll accept that I'm stuck here with you, but don't think we're going to relive our happy home from years past." She rose to her full five-foot-eight-inch height. "Your death is something I had learned to live with. I was moving on, making plans.

"Knowing it was a lie feels like my heart is breaking all over again. That is something I haven't even begun to wrap my mind around. And I may never get over."

"You're my wife, and I will do what is necessary to protect you."

"I don't need a protector. I need a partner. I want what I was to you all the years we were together. Either catch up to the times or get lost again." She turned, stalking into the house and leaving me sprawled on the grass.

8

JAYNA

THE FURY I FELT AS I STALKED INTO THE HOUSE WAS BEYOND anything I could comprehend. I wanted to punch him. I wanted to cry. I wanted to scream. I wanted to run.

I stopped in the middle of what was supposed to be my dream house—the beautiful, giant vacation home with its enormous windows and views of the water.

I saw the array of wine glasses in a cabinet and felt the urge to destroy everything.

I braced my hands on the counter, trying to breathe through the anger.

No, those were the reactions of the Jayna of the past. The girl who rebelled against authority. The girl who never felt a sense of security under the roof of the man who raised her. The girl who needed just one person in the world to put her first.

Nausea filled my stomach, and I placed a palm over my abdomen.

When I'd woken in the giant bed, in the bedroom I'd designed, an indescribable panic had filled me. I'd even thought for a split second Kir was dead, and I'd trapped myself in that place I'd worked so hard to escape.

Then I'd remembered the escapades of the early hours of the morning and rage filled me. At Kir and myself.

How could I have slept with him? Not just once, but three fucking times.

We'd always had this chemistry on a visceral level. And it seemed even now, with all of this pain and anger, I wanted him, craved him.

God, I wanted to hate him so much.

He said he was in a dark place. I knew what dark places were. I'd lost my husband. I'd lost my child. I'd lost even more than that.

If there was one thing I had proven over and over again, it was that I could handle going to hell and back.

And Kir took my choice to handle his hell from me.

Logically, I knew what trauma could do to a person's psyche. But I needed Kir so much and he hadn't been there when he could have.

I had to get answers. But to get answers, I had to keep my temper in check.

Otherwise, Kir would do that damn calm-mode thing he'd just done, which irritated me to no end. Something that in the past resulted in us fucking to get rid of the energy before we finally sat down to have a real discussion.

No more sex. I'd gone nearly three years without it. I could resist him.

Who was I kidding? Even after three marathon rounds of sex, my body ached for his touch.

I turned to look out the kitchen window and found Kir leaning against the half wall at the end of the terrace. He gazed out at the water, lost in thought.

He was still so handsome. He had no idea the change in him made him even more appealing than before. The scars on his face tore at my heart, but repulsion was the last thing I felt. They meant he survived.

In the past, he'd had this perfection about him. What his brothers like to tease and call his cover-model good looks. Now he had an edge, something that made you pause because he was sexy in the viciously dangerous way.

His body was still a work of art, but now more muscular, not as lean. It also told me he trained more with Nik than Sam or Rey. Nik fought like a boxer, and Sam and Rey moved and sparred like mixed martial artists.

When I'd told Kir I wasn't the same person he left behind, I wasn't lying. I loved the life I'd had with him. The woman I used to be needed his protection, needed him to be my knight in shining armor, needed him to be the beast saving me from the evil outside. When he died, I had to learn to stand on my own two feet.

Yes, I'd had help. First, it was Danika, when she took over my gallery and stood as a buffer between Papa and me. Then there was Sylvia Thanos. A woman I affectionately call *Yia Yia Sylvia*. She was a very good client of the gallery who happened to be an eccentric billionaire with her hands in everything, legal and illegal. Sylvia tended to take in lost souls, heal them, and then send them out into the world again.

And she'd done her magic on me.

About a year and a half ago, she'd invited me to her home in the Greek Isles for an extended visit. I'd resisted, and then not six months later, she'd shown up with her private jet and all but forced me onto her plane. She'd treated me like a granddaughter and made me accept the fact that life goes on, and I was ten times stronger than I believed. Her tough love showed me that I could stand on my own and be my own woman.

With Kir back in the picture, I may have to change plans, but I wouldn't go back to the way things were between us.

My fingertips grazed the diamonds of my wedding band.

God. I was still married.

Something deep in me knew that was why I'd resisted taking off the rings. Nearly three years, and I couldn't bring myself to do it.

And now that I'd finally decided to dip my toes into the dating world, this happened.

Oh fuck. Luke.

That was another problem I was going to have to handle. What the hell was I going to tell him?

Sorry, Luke. You see, my dead husband? Well, he's not dead, after all.

Fuck, fuck, fuck. I had a date with Luke tonight, and he would think I'd stood him up.

I looked around the kitchen for anything that would give me access to the outside. Kir had to have a computer or a phone. He always worked in the kitchen. He was a creature of habit.

Wake up before dawn, have coffee at the breakfast table, work on the laptop.

Then all of a sudden, I paused.

Would he put it in the same spot in this house?

Rushing to the dining table, I stooped down and found both Kir's laptop and his cell on a concealed shelf.

Bingo.

Grabbing his phone, I stared at it for a moment.

I could text Sylvia, and she would get me off the island by evening at the latest, or I could dial Danika and give her an ass-chewing.

When I'd told Kir I didn't need his protection, I wasn't lying. By becoming one of Sylvia's girls, as she liked to call us, I could draw on her resources at any time. This was the same as Danika having Solon at her back.

I knew what I had to do. Stay and get my answers. After that, I'd deal with my family.

Kings were supposed to stick together. Kings never betrayed each other. Kings stood by one another through thick and thin.

Pushing down the pain, I dialed Danika.

"Kir. Is she okay? Did they hurt her?" Danika's panicked voiced came over the line.

"*She*," I emphasized, "is fine. Besides a few bruises and a heart filled with complete betrayal."

"J-Jay. I'm so sorry, Jay. I wanted to tell you. Please believe me. I swear. I just didn't know how."

I wanted to believe her. She was the closest thing I had to a sister. We'd been each other's confidantes from the moment Papa had brought Danika into our house after her father's death.

"How long have you known?"

The answer to this would tell me so much about our relationship. Whether I could ever trust Danika again.

"Seven months. The day you decided to move to Miami permanently. I thought Kir was a ghost haunting Nik's apartment, and then one day I threw a letter opener in the direction of the noise and it hit him."

So that's what Kir meant about Danika stabbing him.

Before I could say anything, she continued, "Jay, I didn't even want to wait after that, but Kir finally decided to get his shit together. He's changed. It's like he's the ol—"

I cut her off, not wanting to hear the rest of her words about Kir, and asked, "You swear that you didn't know before then? Not when the accident happened? Or after the mugging, when I lost the baby?"

I pressed my hand over the scars on my stomach.

"I swear. I wouldn't do that to you. I would never let anyone put you through that. I would have made Nik tell you from the beginning, even when Kir couldn't tell you." I could hear the tears in Danika's voice. "Do you really think I would have let you cry yourself to sleep every night as you did, knowing Kir was alive?"

I released a relieved breath, pushing back the memories. I would not go there.

"I believe you," I whispered. "Being here with Kir is too much. I can't think."

"I wouldn't expect anything less."

"Dani, what would you do if you were in my situation?"

"Do you think you can forgive him?"

"I don't know. It's all so fresh, so raw."

"Do you love him?"

"I want to hate him." I knew I hadn't answered her question, but I couldn't say the words.

She was silent for a little bit and then said, "Hear what he has to say and then make your decision. I'll support you, no matter what."

"Even if I decide that I don't want to be with him?"

"Even then."

I swallowed the lump in my throat. "Thanks, Dani."

"I will always have your back. Just do me a favor and don't do anything rash."

"Oh, you mean like fucking the husband I thought was dead? Already did that. Three damn times, in fact."

"Umm. I was thinking more like shooting Kir, but at least you finally got some. Go you."

I would have laughed if I wasn't so mad at myself for letting my hormones get the best of me.

"I already tried that too."

"You've been busy."

"Yep." I released a deep breath. "Tell me what's going on. I can't keep my temper when I'm around Kir, and I need answers."

"I've tracked the contracts to third-party freelancers. I'm still working on one of them. Whoever they hired to hide their tracks is good. But I'm better, and I'll find them."

"Dani, it's Papa. He's the one with the most to gain by taking me or eliminating me."

"I wouldn't be so sure it's him. He knows I'll come after him, and right now, he's too wrapped up in his political career. He looks clean. His partners are another question. They may do things on his behalf, so I'll dive in there. Right now, I need you to answer a serious question and don't lie to me."

"Okay, what?"

"What did you do to piss off Hector Estefan?"

Why would she bring him up? I had nothing to do with that part of Kir's family.

"Kir's cousin, that Hector Estefan?"

"Yes, that one. You know, the mafia boss."

"I have no fucking idea."

"Jay, I know you do all that shit with assets and your companies to hide the lineage of ownership. I never ask what you are up to since those are your secrets. You either worked with or did something to get on Hector's radar. He was in Miami yesterday, and you were supposed to be the extra passenger on his plane."

"Dani, the only people I piss off on a regular basis are those in the fight world and Papa. The last person I pissed off was, in fact, Papa." I paced and then stopped as a thought came to me. "Oh shit, Dani."

"What? Don't leave me hanging."

"The shell company partner. The one I set up while I was in Greece."

When I'd created the Ladai Room clubs, I'd established them under the guise of a silent partnership. A partnership on paper only. With the name buried so deep, they would have to trace through four different companies and three trusts across the US and Europe to find the name.

I'd worked in the fight business long enough to know having an investor who was male, even if they remained in the shadows, gave me the clout I needed to run my business without interference. I'd made it known I had a partner but never disclosed who it was, letting the rumor mill and the notoriety of my connection to the Kings keep people guessing.

Yes, it fucking sucked to have to play stupid underhanded games, but it was the way it was in a male-dominated industry. And if anyone ever went looking, it would take dedicated effort to uncover my silent partner's name.

"You mean the penis partner? Please tell me you didn't pick a name tied to Kir."

I clenched my teeth and said, "I wouldn't be in this situation if someone bothered to tell me my husband was alive."

"In other words, you picked something that would make Hector believe Kir hadn't died in the crash. And with you moving to Miami and hiring out Kir's family, it looks as if Kir is setting up his territory."

"I run clubs. It has nothing to do with the King business structure."

"Get real. Until recently, you ran illegal fight clubs in addition to your nightclubs. And I'm sure Nik talked you into running some of his favors through your establishments a time or two. You aren't Mrs. Straight-and-Narrow."

"I still run the clubs, Dani. But I hear what you're saying." I sighed. "Shit. I'm going to have to tell Kir."

"He probably already knows. Rey's digging, and the brothers were holed up in Nik's office this morning working on some master plan. I haven't had a chance to talk to Nik to get the details."

"I guess I'm stuck here." I closed my eyes and pressed my fingers to the bridge of my nose. "I hate not having control of my life. I've worked too hard to go backward."

"Then don't let that temper of yours win. Kir isn't Uncle. You have to remember that."

"I don't know what to do. My emotions are riding me. I don't want to be that person who reacts or lashes out. I lived a lifetime in that place. I'm not that person anymore."

"I know it isn't fair, but you have a lot of decisions on your shoulders."

"That's an understatement."

At that moment, I heard the sound of the glass sliding doors of the patio open, and I turned to face Kir as he walked in.

He shook his head and a slight smile touched his lips.

"I'll call you when I get home. Right now, I need to get some answers from my not-dead husband."

"Is he standing before you?"

"Yep."

"To be a fly on the wall in that house right now. You're probably either fighting or fucking."

"Yep," was all I said as I held Kir's gaze.

Danika laughed. "I love you, Jay. And don't ever forget, I'm always on your side. You're my sister."

A warmth washed over me. "I love you too."

I slid the phone from my ear and set it on the counter.

"So, you found my hiding place." Kir took a step toward me.

I ignored the tingle in the pit of my stomach that grew as he came closer. "It's not much of a hiding place."

"Am I that predictable?"

"It seems that way."

"And is Dani helping you leave since you said you would call her when you got home?"

I narrowed my eyes. "I'm eventually getting home, aren't I?"

He came forward until he had me trapped between him and the sink.

"You are home." Setting a hand on either side of me, he leaned forward. "You're the one who designed this place."

"My home is where I say it is. This is not it." I held his gaze, trying to ignore how amazing he smelled and the way his naked chest grazed against the fabric covering my nipples.

"And this home of yours." His voice grew husky with lust. "Is there a place for me there?"

The desire cleared from my mind as pain replaced it. "I don't know yet. I'm not sure I can trust you."

"What will make you trust me again?"

"You can start by telling me this plan Dani said you and the guys are working on. Then we'll see where we go from there."

"You want to hear our plan?"

"I wouldn't have said it if I didn't mean it."

"Kiran Antoni King, or should I say, Antoni Silva, is coming back from the dead and claiming what belongs to him."

9

KIRAN

"ARE YOU INSANE?" THE OUTRAGE ON HER FACE WAS SOMETHING I hadn't expected. "You can't just walk back into the world and say, "Hey everyone, I didn't die like you thought I did."

"Princesa, you already set up the legwork for me. Isn't Antoni Silva the silent partner in all of the Ladai Room locations?"

The fact I'd used the Antoni Silva name twice now without her reacting meant she suspected we'd figured out her secret.

"That was buried. How did you discover the name so fast?"

"Danika isn't the only hacker in the family. Though I can admit Rey isn't as good as her, he is still considered an expert in the field. Plus, he has connections that could boggle the mind."

Ever since Danika had found chatter about the contracts on Jayna's abduction, I had Rey dive deep into Jayna's business to see if she'd made enemies while setting up her Ladai Room clubs.

She'd gone into an occupation dominated by men and usually by those with underhanded tactics. The fact she'd succeeded with her concept and made what tended to be an illegal and usually underground operation into something legal would have pissed off more than a few people.

What surprised everyone the most was that under layer after layer of trusts and shell corporations was the name of her silent partner.

Me.

Well, Antoni Silva.

She'd created a whole persona with businesses and tax records. She'd used the skills she'd learned under Danika's tutelage, and no one was the wiser.

No, that wasn't true.

By picking Silva, she'd triggered Hector's interest. If he'd had any clue that I was still alive, this would have made him believe it was true.

Anyone and everyone knew Jayna was my weakness. Targeting her was the fastest way to get me out of the shadows.

She lifted her chin. "I did what was necessary. The fight club business is misogynistic. If I let the rumor mill believe I had an anonymous partner with a penis, then people would leave me alone. No one needed the name. It was more the penis part."

The spark of defiance that lit up her amber eyes had my cock jumping and gave me visions of bending her over the counter and fucking her senseless.

Yes, I should never forget Jayna knew her way around a computer. Hell, it was her mastery of business, international law, and the cyber world that gave her the edge in creating the Silva persona.

"Well, I have news for you. Antoni Silva is real, and he does have a penis." I moved forward, pressing my cock into her belly. "How long have you been able to forge my signature?"

She licked her lips, and her cheeks flushed as she set her hands on my chest.

Suddenly, a flash of sadness washed over her face before she schooled it away in anger. "When I picked the name, you were dead."

"I'm so sorry, baby. I promise I will make it up to you."

"We'll see."

I knew I deserved that. Trust. I'd broken her trust, and I had to earn it back.

"You will." I ran a thumb over her lower lip. "You didn't answer my question."

"It's not exactly your signature, but close."

"Close enough that even Rey thought it looked like my handwriting."

"I mastered forging my father's signature long before we met. How do you think I got out of so many of the school activities he insisted would make me a proper lady?"

"Why don't I know this about you? I thought I knew everything."

"There is a lot you don't know about me, Kir. Especially now." The fire was back in her amber gaze, telling me I was about to step on some landmines.

"Then let me get to know the Jayna Shah King of today."

"Are you sure you want to get to know her? You may not like her. She doesn't need you to complete her anymore."

I would take every barb she threw at me if it meant I had her in the end.

"But I need her to complete me."

"If that were true, we wouldn't be in this situation."

Pushing me back, Jayna walked into the living room, slid onto the oversized couch and tucked her feet next to her, then ordered, "Sit."

I knew this Jayna. This was the no-nonsense woman who was about to become all business. She'd go into this mode whenever she'd arrange the matches for our fights. No one fucked with her when she was in this mood.

Following her directions, I took the lounger across from her.

"It's time to lay everything on the table. No more secrets. No more hiding. Then I can decide if there is even a chance that I can trust you again."

"What about your secrets?"

"Those you'll have to earn."

Fucking hell, this side of her turned me on like nothing else.

Jayna folded her arms across her chest and leaned back on the sofa. "I want the details of this plan. But first, I need you to put all the pieces together of the past. I feel as if I missed so much. And maybe it was my fault for letting you be my shield for so long. I'm not that woman anymore. I need all the facts."

"I think I need a drink first." I went over to a cabinet filled with liquor, poured myself a large helping of scotch, and then threw it back, letting the liquid burn down my throat and settle in my stomach.

After refilling my glass and filling a glass of whiskey over ice for Jayna, I returned to the living room, handing Jayna the tumbler.

I took my seat and asked, "Do you remember around the time of your six-month checkup when I had to leave to collect on a breached favor?"

She nodded.

"Well, someone put out a few contracts on me in the open market. None of us had taken them seriously since shit like that happened all the time when we had to collect from the idiots. And usually, they disappeared as fast as they appeared.

"This time, they stayed active. In the process of Rey and our team trying to figure out who put the hit out on me, I focused all my energy into making sure you and our baby were safe."

"That's why the only time you ever left me alone was when I was at the gallery. You should have told me."

I should have told her a lot of things.

"On the night of my accident, one of the contracts was executed. I'd felt something was off the whole day, but I still got in that damn car because I wanted to be the one to pick you up."

"And instead, I got the call from Dani." Jayna's hands shook as she drank the whiskey. "Keep going."

"This is based on what the guys told me. The reason they lied to you was that the contract wasn't complete without a body. Nik and his team had arrived and moved me before anyone could physically confirm my death."

"But the video. I saw the video."

"The footage your father had may have satisfied him and his partners, but not the people who executed the hit. In their world, no body means not dead. So they went looking for me and broke into Nik's building, thinking the guys stashed me there.

"At the time, my brothers didn't know about the footage Shah had. They were going on instinct and the need to keep me alive and you safe. They thought if they made you believe I was gone, then others would too.

"Your mugging took everyone by surprise. The guys thought you were safe with your two-person security team. In our business, wives and children are off-limits. Anyone who breaks this rule faces dire consequences."

"Papa isn't in your world," Jayna said in an almost detached voice, a tone I'd never heard before. "Dani traced it to someone connected to Papa's circle of friends but couldn't pinpoint exactly who it was."

"It's a significant possibility it's your boyfriend's father."

I couldn't help but clench my teeth thinking about Lukesh Joshi having the privilege to spend time with Jayna. It was torture watching him flirt with her, laugh with her, going out in public with her. I felt as if someone had lodged a knife in my heart and left it there. The only consolation I had was the fact Jayna had never taken off her wedding bands.

Jayna narrowed her gaze instead of seeming surprised by my statement. "Luke isn't his father. And for the record, he isn't my boyfriend. Our first date was supposed to be tonight. I guess your spying didn't get you that information."

Ignoring her jab, I said, "He's the heir to the family. Don't underestimate him."

"He's my friend."

Yeah, a friend who wanted in her pants.

"Your safety was always a factor in every decision everyone

made. That contract on me never closed, Jayna. They revised it to state you were now acceptable collateral damage if it led them to me."

"Are you expecting me to believe that you pretended to be dead to protect me?" She set her tumbler down on the side table and clenched her fist.

"Yes and no." I gripped the back of my head. "It wasn't about the contract. That was something you understood from the beginning. We could have put precautions in place for that."

"Then what was it?"

"I was a living nightmare. I would have brought more danger into your life being the person I was."

"What does that mean?"

"When you hear about people recovering from horrific accidents, they talk about the physical, but they rarely discuss the mental aspect of it." I stared into Jayna's eyes and said, "I broke, Jayna. The pain was too much to handle. I drank, took meds to a level where I became a raging addict, and lived in anger. I was supposed to be the strong one, the enforcer, and I couldn't even get out of a chair without help. I was a shell of the man you knew."

"You don't just snap out of that place. What truly got you to where you are now?"

"You're right. It wasn't one thing. The guys kept telling me it was time to get my shit together. They physically forced me into rehab, going as far as making it all but impossible for me to check myself out. Once I detoxed, I started seeing a therapist.

"But the real push came when you came back from Greece and decided to leave New York. I knew Sylvia had done her magic, and you were ready to move on. It wasn't Dani finding out. It was knowing I'd have to live without you forever if I didn't make a change."

Jayna rose and started pacing. "Are you saying that I was the catalyst for your healing? And you couldn't be bothered to tell me you were alive?"

She stopped moving and glared at me with anger and a sheen of tears in her eyes. "Fuck. That. Shit."

She stalked toward me, and I stood, bracing for whatever she had for me. "I had a right to decide what I could and couldn't handle. We made vows to each other. Did they mean anything to you?"

"They meant everything to me."

She shoved me.

"Bullshit. I needed you. Just knowing you were there would have made a difference. I wouldn't have…" Jayna trailed off, biting her lip and closing her eyes for a brief second.

"What aren't you telling me?"

"It doesn't matter." She shook her head. "What I'd like to know is how you are planning to fix this. Are you going to hide away again? Or are you going to man up? I fought for you the first time. If you want me in your life, then you're going to have to fight for me."

"That's the plan."

"You think stepping into the role of a fictional person I created is going to show you're fighting for me?"

"Antoni Silva isn't fictional. He is very real. The name on my birth certificate before Arin had it changed was Kiran Antoni Silva. I'm the heir to the Silva Familia, according to my paternal grandfather, Victor Silva.

"By picking that name, you jumped onto Hector's radar. It

doesn't matter how deep you try to bury things. When it comes to threats to his business, he is going to find out."

"That still doesn't answer how casting yourself into the role of Antoni Silva is going to do anything other than place a giant target on your back."

"That's the point. Hector comes directly for me. I want to end this shit with him once and for all. And if it means confronting him and settling the shit my grandfather created, so be it."

"And how do I play into this?"

"It's going to give me the cover I need to get to know you as you are now, to date you, to show you we are worth saving."

She studied me, not saying anything for a few seconds. "So, I'm going from a King's wife to a mobster's girlfriend?"

I set a hand on her waist. "Some would say that you already have experience in that role."

As a King, people put us in the same category as those in the underworld, but we were far from it. Everyone needed favors, from the upstanding Wall Street boys, who needed extra loans to cover debts about to be called, to the syndicate bosses who wanted to enter the world of the Hamptons elite. We just brokered the deals to accomplish their goals and collected favors in exchange.

"You really think I'm going to make it that easy?"

I smirked, resisting the urge to draw her toward me and kiss her. "Jay, you're going to make me work for every scrap you throw my way."

She stepped out of my hold and moved to the mantel where I'd placed a frame containing our wedding picture.

It was on the beach in Tahiti. Jayna wore a simple strapless white gown, and I had on a button-down shirt with a pair of linen slacks. It was perfect and just the two of us. We'd decided to elope instead of dealing with the chaos of a wedding that would cause endless headaches for Jayna and her mother.

She traced the frame and then said, "You broke my heart. Why should I even give you a chance? Why should I even go through with this plan?"

"Because you're my everything, and I want to prove it to you. I know I fucked up. If I could do it all again, I would have demanded Nik brought you to me when I learned they'd told you I'd died. Maybe I wouldn't have gone down the path I had."

There were so many times I'd wondered if Jayna had known I was alive, would I have lost my way. Would I have become the monster my brothers had to bring back from the point of self-destruction?

"But you can't."

"I can't. All I can do is hope you can forgive me."

"You're going to have to call in a lot of favors to make Antoni Silva a living person. The man only exists on paper."

"It's already in the works. This morning while you slept, I met with the guys. They began the process of making sure Antoni Silva has a footprint of running a lucrative import-export business out of Florida. Within the next few weeks, everyone will know one of Victor Silva's grandsons has claimed Miami as his home base."

Jayna turned to face me. "Are you sure you can handle it? You don't like being in public. You're more of a behind-the-scenes kind of man. Do you remember how long it took you to get used to being with a socialite? The only place you ever liked attention was in the cage."

"I can handle it. I'm not going to lie and say it's something I want to do, especially looking like this." I gestured to my face. "But if there is a chance it will fix things between us, then I'm going to do it. Besides, before you, voyeuristic sex was never on my radar and since it got you off, I did it."

Jayna narrowed her gaze. "It's not as if you didn't get off at the same time."

"True, but it's not my vice." I took a step toward her. "I mean it, Princesa. I'd chase you across the world if that's what it takes."

"And protecting me is a secondary thing?"

"Protecting you is never secondary. It just comes with the territory. We can assume your father or one of his associates was behind the second hit on you yesterday. Now we have to find out what they want."

"I won't let you put me in a cage, Kir."

"Jayna, even before my accident, you weren't the type of woman to ever let anyone put you in a cage. It won't be anything more than you'd expect—increased security and the normal itinerary notifications."

"You've got it all planned out, I see." She took a deep breath. "Anything else you need to lay out on the table, so I'm not slapped in the face by another surprise?"

"The cleanup I called in the favor on. Solon did it."

"What? Are you saying you work for them?"

"Not quite. But let's say the skills I learned from Arin are useful in other capacities as well."

"What exactly do you do for them?"

I lifted a brow. "You tell me what you and Danika do for them, and I will do the same."

"Hack." She pursed her lips in a "that was a stupid question" way and then continued, "You already knew this. Besides, as an insider, wouldn't you already have access to the details on our projects?"

"Available information at Solon is based on assignment, just like any other organization. Only a few have all the details. It keeps people safer."

"Understandable. How long have you worked for them?"

"As I said, I don't work for them. I provide my services to them and other agencies."

She glared at me. "Same thing. Answer the question."

"Since the time we met."

"I see. Did you think I couldn't handle that too? I fucking married you, knowing what you did for a living. Dammit, Kir. I never kept secret the fact I work for them on projects with Danika."

"Your job was behind a computer and mine was the exact opposite. You trusted me to protect you. I wasn't going to bring fear into your life after what you dealt with under your father's rule."

"I don't need you to shelter me anymore. I'm not that barely twenty-year-old girl who needed a prince to rescue her. I'm not even that twenty-eight-year-old you knew before the accident. I've lived a lifetime since then."

"You still need protection."

"A security detail is adequate for my protection. I've had one everywhere I go."

"So yesterday was the exception, or did you try to lose them on your way to your mother's as you usually do?"

She sighed. "Look. It's a stupid game I've played with them

for years. They're good. I can never lose them for more than a minute, two at the most."

"Two minutes that nearly had you kidnapped."

She cocked her head to the side and then narrowed her eyes. "Where were they during the abduction? They should have gotten to me before anything went down."

"The abductors knew your routine, Jayna. They knew everyone in your detail and targeted them to slow them down. They coordinated every aspect of the abduction down to the second. The only thing that fucked them up was the second party and me."

"What does my team think happened to me?"

"My security lead made sure they were fine after the abduction attempt and then informed them you're safe and with me. Currently the teams are coordinating the logistics on ways to make your return as smooth as possible."

"Isn't it nice how you wrapped everything up in a big bow for me?" The fire was back in her amber eyes.

"I will do what is necessary to protect you."

"Listen very clearly. You want to be a part of my life. Then what I need is a companion, a lover, a partner who thinks of me as an equal, not someone who wants to wrap me in cotton as if I would break. I've proven I won't break. Either step up or disappear again. I have a life to get back to and plans of my own to fulfill."

Breathing heavily, she moved to the side table, picked up her drink, and swallowed it in one large gulp. She closed her eyes as the liquid slid down her throat.

There was no winning this. I had to break the walls she'd erected and to do this, I had to give her what she wanted.

"And what will make you believe I see who you are now?"

"Your actions." Her hazel gaze bored into mine as if daring me and not believing I could do it.

"Does that mean you'll go along with the plan?"

"For the time being. You will not make decisions for me ever again. Is that clear?"

When we'd gotten together, she'd had this hard shell around her—constantly fighting to get what she wanted, defying any form of authority.

I'd been so cruel to her then, telling her to go back to her ivory tower and her charmed life. My only excuse was that the moment our eyes had connected during my match, I'd felt something, and I knew she was out of my league. Then after the match, when she'd come with her friends to talk to me, I'd seen the designer clothes on her body and the diamonds in her ears and believed she was just slumming it for kicks.

Over the next few weeks, she kept coming back, especially on the nights I was on the ticket to fight. She'd even worked her way into my circle of friends.

Her determination drew me like a moth to a flame. She'd gotten under my skin like no other woman before. Even then, I resisted. I was a twenty-two-year-old idiot.

Then one night, I'd found her curled up in a ball, hiding in one of the back rooms of the club. She'd had bruises on her arms and a black eye. A frightened, shattered woman sat in the place of the tough-as-nails debutante I'd gotten so used to seeing.

It had taken nearly an hour to get her to tell me her father had beaten her and that it hadn't been the first time.

Every protective instinct I'd had in my body had surged

forward, and I knew I'd never let anyone hurt Jayna again. Protecting her at all costs had become my mission, both physically and mentally.

God, I'd fucked up on both accounts.

Jayna spoke, drawing my attention back to her. "Nothing to say?"

"Oh, I have a lot to say."

She lifted a brow. "Go on."

"First, protecting you is something that comes naturally to me." She opened her mouth to argue, but I spoke again. "But I hear you. You have your security detail. You aren't stupid and you know what's at stake, especially with what happened yesterday."

"Go on."

"Second, I will keep you in the loop on everything that concerns you. Antoni Silva's deals will remain his. Just like I stayed out of your club businesses, and you kept out of King Holding activities, the same applies here."

She pursed her lips but nodded. "Anything else?"

"Yes, we will date. This way, I get to know you outside of the bedroom."

"Can I assume that means no sex?"

She thought she was funny. Sex was something she wanted as much as I did. Hell, she was the one who'd ordered me to fuck her in the bathroom.

"You tell me."

She licked her lips as her gaze went to mine. "We'll just have to see how impressive you are with this dating thing."

"Then the plan is a go."

"As I said, for now. I have a right to change my mind if you piss me off."

"Fair enough."

Her gaze went to the glass doors leading into the sunroom with a large hanging sofa swing. "Since I'm stuck here for the time being, I'm going to explore the house I designed."

"This is your house. You don't need my permission."

"That's right. I don't." She moved past me and toward the sunroom, leaving me to stare after her.

If this was the first step in breaking down the giant wall between us, so be it.

10

JAYNA

"What do you want for dinner?" Kir asked me as I came down the staircase leading into the kitchen.

Dear God. Every time I heard him speak, my heart clenched.

He was real.

He was mine.

Well, maybe he was. We still had so far to go.

Trust was a big issue right now. So many people had broken my trust. And agreeing to the plan meant I would have to deal with everyone in time.

After exploring the house, I'd gotten Kir to thoroughly detail the plans for when we left the island. I couldn't believe what Kir was going to go through to become Antoni Silva. He'd become this very public, very seen but unseen persona. It scared me a bit that people might recognize him, but Kir insisted he had it covered.

My role in this whole thing was to live my life, and when the time came, he would appear as my partner, and we'd start dating.

He made it sound so simple. Nothing was ever that simple.

"Your options are halibut or chicken," Kir continued, bringing me back to his question.

"I'll go with halibut." I took the last step and stopped as Kir came into sight.

Holy fuck.

Kir leaned over a cookbook. Shirtless. Every inch of his honed, sculpted upper body was that of a warrior. My fingers itched to trace those tattoos. Hell, I wanted to explore all of him.

God, those incredible muscled abs that led down into the V that ended at the drawstring of his lounge pants.

When my perusal went back to Kir's face, his gaze was molten lava.

We stared at each other. There was no denying the pull. All I wanted was to touch him. To kiss those lips, to taste them, to lose myself in them.

Why hadn't he kissed me?

In the past, we'd spent so much time just exploring with our mouths. And damn, did Kir have an incredible one.

I wanted to reach out and run my fingers across his plump lower lip.

Get it together, Jayna.

I wasn't supposed to let my hormones rule me and let this attraction toward him drag me back in.

"Stop looking at me like that. Remember, you wanted me to get to know the Jayna of today. I'm supposed to impress you with my dating skills."

I said nothing, just continued to stare at him. My mind and my body were at war, and it was better to remain silent.

"I mean it. What happened this morning barely scratched the surface of my desires, and you aren't ready for what I want to do."

I licked my lips as my breaths grew shallow, and before I thought better of it, I asked, "What do you want to do?"

"I want to fuck every part of you." He shifted around the counter, coming closer. "Your mouth, your cunt, your ass."

Everything inside me clenched at the visions of doing all those things with him—the unrestrained rawness of it.

When it came to my body, I'd never denied him anything. He knew me inside and out, my needs, my desires. He never let me hide anything. My craving for him was visceral, almost uncontrollable. Always had been and probably would never change.

"That requires my permission."

"The way your body is reacting to me, I have no doubt you'd give it."

"Perhaps," I admitted, resulting in a slight curve to his lips.

"There is no perhaps about it, Princesa."

Ignoring the way his use of my nickname sent tingles down my spine instead of annoying me, I asked, "Are you serious about chasing me across the world, if that's what it takes?"

He stopped in front of me. "Are you planning to run?"

"It's a possibility."

"Then I should tell you." He leaned down, his mouth a hairsbreadth from mine. "I will come after you."

"Good to know." Without thought, I lifted my face to kiss him, but he pulled away, making me frown.

Had he just done that on purpose?

"Why did you avoid kissing me?"

"Because kissing you means something to me. It means something to us. You were the one who told me kisses were special."

I'd said those words over eleven years ago when I'd been so young, barely twenty years old.

Kir had found me hiding in his gym after I'd run from my father following a fight where he'd used his fist to make a point on how I was an utter disappointment to him and our family name. Papa had wanted me to honor a business agreement he'd made with Luke's father to marry Luke after graduating college and I'd refused.

Kir had nearly lost it, seeing the bruises on my face and arms. But, instead of going after Papa as I'd expected, he'd tended to me and promised me that I never had to see Papa again unless I absolutely wanted to.

Up until then, he'd made me believe I was a pest, constantly chasing after him. I hadn't realized he actually cared for me or knew that I didn't have the perfect princess life that he kept saying I lived.

"If I kiss you, the same thing I said back then will hold true now."

The second my lips touch yours, you will belong to me. There is no going back. Life as you know it will never be the same.

"You want me to belong to you, Kir?"

"You already do."

"Then why did you avoid the kiss?"

"Because I want you to accept it."

That was something that was not going to happen.

"The old Jayna belonged body, mind, and soul to Kiran King. Until you get to know the woman who is standing before you, she is willing to give you her body, but the rest, you'll have to earn."

"Then I guess we won't be kissing."

"Then I guess we won't." I pivoted, motioning to go into the living room, but he grabbed my hand, pulling me against him.

"You just said you're willing to give me your body. Well, I'm going to take full advantage of it."

"What happened to the dating?"

"Oh, we're going to date, but that's after we leave this island." He threaded his fingers in my hair, tilting my face up, almost as if his lips were going to brush mine, and then rubbed his stubble-covered jaw along mine. "Are you willing, Jayna? It's your call."

I clutched at his arms as his teeth scraped along the vein on my throat, making me crave more and have visions of things we'd done in the past.

I knew better. Sex was only going to complicate things further. I wasn't even sure we had a future.

God, I was a mess.

Why did he smell so good?

Oh, hell with it.

"I want you to fuck me, Kir."

"With pleasure."

He backed me up against the island, sandwiching my body between him and the stone.

"Yes," I moaned, arching into the brush of his mouth on my shoulder.

He lifted his head and looked into my eyes. "I plan to feast on you tonight. It may take some time to set everything in motion."

"You sound as if we aren't going to see each other for months."

"That's a possibility."

I frowned. How was he planning on dating me?

Before I could ask my question, he continued. "Will you miss me, Princesa? After all, we've only been back together for a little over twenty-four hours."

My fingers flexed against his chest. Underneath all the anger was the fear he wouldn't come back again.

I wouldn't voice it. I wouldn't let him see that vulnerability. Needing him in that way was something I couldn't risk again.

"I will come back," Kir said as if reading my thoughts. "No more hiding."

I studied him, wanting to believe him, feeling the draw of him.

After a few moments, I whispered, "We'll see."

"You will see," he said, fire and determination in his gaze.

Just as he was about to shift, I stayed him by cupping his face. "Let me touch you."

He nodded, and I slowly traced my fingers from his left temple where the scar started and over the corner of his eye. It amazed me that he could still see. Then I touched along his stubble-covered jaw, down his neck, over his tattooed shoulders, before moving back up again.

"I like how this gives you that dangerous edge. It's sexy as hell," I said, looking into his beautiful eyes.

"I'm glad you think so." He turned his face into my palm, kissing the center.

"I know so." I stood on tiptoes, and without thinking, went to brush my lips against his, but he shifted his face.

I pushed down the pang of disappointment. Kir wanted something from me that I wasn't willing to give him. I might never give him.

As if sensing my warring thoughts, Kir pulled me toward him and slowly undressed me. First, he removed my shirt, then my pants, followed by my bra and underwear.

When I stood before him completely bare, I was almost transported back to a time before all the pain and the deception when we were so young and driven by our passion and need.

"You're the one who's sexy as hell." He raked me with his heated gaze, causing my nipples to strain into tight buds and goosebumps to prickle down my skin.

I'd always had a curvier body, a body I'd grown to love and accept after leaving my father's house. But it wasn't until Kir that I had a man touch me as if fuller breasts and hips were something to worship.

"Kir," I whimpered. "Do something."

He came toward me, cupping my aching breasts. "Shouldn't you start calling me Antoni? That's who's going to make love to you when I get to Miami."

"The only man touching me is you. Kir and Antoni are the

same. You said so yourself." I arched up as he pinched the straining buds of my nipples.

The pressure grew harder, making me gasp.

"Are you sure about that? The public is going to believe otherwise." He slid a hand around my waist and lifted me onto the hard surface of the island. "You're about to become Antoni Silva's woman."

I cupped his face, staring into the dark depths of his eyes. "You will always be Kir to me. When we're together, it's Kiran and Jayna."

"Do Kiran and Jayna still exist?" He collared my throat with his fingers, making my heartbeat spike and arousal flood my core. "Or is it just sexual attraction?"

He pushed me back until I was lying flat on the granite.

Just as I parted my lips to answer, he spread my knees apart, and his warm breath grazed the insides of my thighs.

The ache deep in my core intensified, and I moaned, "Kir," as I gazed up at our reflection through the glass of the skylight. Kir was fully dressed, and I was completely naked and open to him.

"I haven't tasted you in years," he said as he hooked my legs around his shoulders and brought me against his mouth. "I've dreamed about it. Fucking craved it."

The first presses of his mouth were soft, too soft for the need growing inside me. My fingers gripped his hair, trying to urge him to where I needed him.

"Hands on the counter, or I'll stop." He blew on my clit a second before licking it and then raised his head, waiting for me to comply.

I released my hold on his hair and placed my fingers on the hard edge of the stone counter.

"All you have to do is enjoy. Let me pleasure you, Princesa. You know how much I love making you come." His lips descended on my clit, sucking it into his mouth, and all coherent thoughts left my head.

"Oh God," I cried out as my back bowed.

He licked, circled, and teased before he moved lower to thrust in and out of my pussy, driving my arousal higher and higher. The muscles deep in my core quivered and flooded with desire.

A satisfied hum came from him as our eyes locked. He knew what he was doing to me, surging my need up until I was desperate and begging.

And dear God, I was ready to beg. Damn Kir and his wicked mouth. How could I have forgotten that vicious mouth of his?

"Kir, please. I need to come."

He slid a finger into my pussy and then curved it, hitting the spot that would send me over. My body immediately responded, and I threw my head back and screamed my release. Kir continued to feast on my pussy for I had no idea how long, keeping me suspended in wave after wave of pleasure.

When Kir finally finished gorging on me, I was nothing but a melted, exhausted pile of limbs. He lifted me in his arms, carried me outside, and then lay down with me on the giant outdoor sofa, my back to his front.

I sighed, loving the sound of the water and the warm breeze gliding over my skin.

"Sleep, baby," he whispered into my hair as he stroked his

fingers down my arm. "I think I've wrung every orgasm out of you for tonight."

The hard press of his cock into my back told me he was in desperate need of relief.

Why hadn't he fucked me?

Lifting my head, I looked at him. "What about you?"

"We have plenty of time. Right now, rest." He closed his eyes and lifted one arm above his head, dropping it back against the arm of the couch.

I settled back along his body and tried to relax but failed as the presence of his thick erection remained between us. A low throbbing deep in my core ignited again, and my skin tingled with need.

Kir's breath changed as if he sensed what was happening to me.

Turning, I braced a hand on either side of him and brought my face an inch away from his.

"Kir," I said.

He lifted his lids, desire clouding his almost black eyes. "Yes."

"I want to ride you."

His hands came to my waist. "This wasn't about me. It was about you."

I smiled down at him, sliding my naked, wet pussy up and down the seam of his pants. His cock grew harder, and his fingers flexed, pressing into my skin.

"This is about me. Don't you think I enjoy seeing you go over? I love watching the muscles of your face tighten and feeling the extra swelling of your thick cock right before you empty inside me."

He swallowed as his pupils ate up his irises, turning them completely black. "If we do this, I'm going to fuck you hard. Are you sure you want to go there?"

I reached between us and cupped his cock, circling the head with the tips of my fingers. "Does it look as if I'm objecting?"

He stared at me for a few moments then said, "Take me out, Jayna."

Oh damn, I loved when his voice got all deep and commanding like that.

Goosebumps prickled my skin as I lifted onto my knees and pulled the drawstring of his pants free before pushing his pants down enough to free his hard, hot length. I gripped him at the base, stroking up and down.

A drop of precum beaded the tip, making me want to lean down and lick it off.

"No. You wanted to ride me. Then ride me."

Oh, I was going to ride him.

Sliding into position, I angled my weeping pussy over his cock. Slowly, inch by inch, I worked him into me. It was a tease for both of us.

My core spasmed with each slide down. When he was finally seated to the hilt, I couldn't help but throw my head back and savor the feel of him inside me. This fullness. I'd missed it.

Kir cupped my breast, drawing my attention to his face. "Do you know how many times I imagined you like this? You're so fucking beautiful."

"Probably the same number of times I've imagined you under me." I set my hands on his chest, not wanting to go down that path.

Instead, I rose up until only the head of his cock sat in my pussy and then slammed back down.

"Fuck," Kir cried out, gripping my leg in an almost painful hold. "If you keep doing that, I'm going to come."

"Kir. I have to move. I...I..." I began a steady rhythm, savoring the incredible feel of him. "So good. Fuck, this is so good."

With each up-and-down slide, his cock hit the sensitive spot that would send me over. I rocked and undulated my hips, getting closer and closer to the peak I was now so desperate to reach.

"Oh Kir. Fuck. I'm so close. I need."

His thumb settled on my clit. "What do you need, baby?"

I continued my movement, lost in the need for release.

"Say it, and I'll help you." He pressed down on the bundle of nerves at the apex of my sex, sending spasms deep into my core.

"Oooh God."

"Nope, that's not it."

I clenched my teeth and then, out of complete desperation, cried out, "Kir, make me come."

"As you wish, Princesa." Kir stroked my clit in that way only he'd ever done.

My rhythm faltered as everything in my body tightened and my core flooded with desire.

"Yes, that's it."

All of a sudden, my mind clouded, and I threw my head back as my pussy clamped down on Kir's cock.

"Kir." I scored my nails down his arms.

I heard Kir hiss, but he continued to play with my clit, drawing out my release.

As I started to come down, I felt his fingers dig into my thighs, and I knew he was about to take over.

"My turn." Kir lifted me off him and then pushed me forward onto the sofa.

I barely had time to register what was happening before he grabbed both of my wrists and pinned them to the hollow of my back.

My pulse jumped, and my breath grew ragged. I wasn't sure how, after the orgasms I'd already had, but the pulsing inside my core started again.

Wedging my knees apart with his, he positioned himself between my legs and rubbed the head of his cock up and down my slick, dripping slit.

I glanced over my shoulder, and the glint I saw in his eyes told me this was going to be hard and fast.

"You ready?" he asked through clenched teeth.

Before I could say anything, Kir thrust in with so much force that the pleasure-pain of it was almost too much to bear.

"Oh God," I gasped, clutching my fingers under the vise grip he had on my wrists.

"I warned you." He pulled out and thrust back in. "Now you have to deal with it."

"I wouldn't have said I wanted it if I didn't."

His hold on my hands intensified and he used my arms to pull me back to meet him as his hips drove forward.

The intensity of this, the feel of this, the rawness of this had my body on fire.

He hammered my pussy with his thick cock as if he was trying to imprint himself on me so hard that he jarred the furniture adjacent to us.

"More," I whimpered. There was no denying that Kir was the only man who ever understood what my body needed, wanted, craved.

He released his hold on my wrists and collared my throat again, pulling me back against him as he continued to thrust in and out of me. My pussy quickened, and my mind clouded.

Yes. I was almost there.

"Is this what you wanted?" He tightened his hold on my neck.

"Yes," I cried out. "Yes. I don't need gentle. I need this."

Dear God. This was what I wanted. The raw, unrestrained Kir.

"I can't hold out any longer." Kir released his hold on my throat and gripped my hips. "Are you with me?"

"I'm with you." I clenched my eyes tight as everything inside me contracted around his pistoning cock.

"Fuck. You're squeezing me so tight… Oh fuck. Jayna…" Kir's pace faltered and he began to come.

The swelling of his cock deep inside me pushed me over the edge into my release, and my back bowed and pleasure overtook me.

11

JAYNA

A LITTLE AFTER TEN IN THE MORNING, I ARRIVED AT A PRIVATE airfield to find my Mercedes parked and waiting for me, exactly as Kir said it would be.

We'd spent most of the night lost in each other, touching, tasting, exploring. We knew there was a time limit to be together, and we took advantage of it.

I could still see his face getting farther and farther away as the boat he'd arranged took me from our island and brought me to the dock, where a security detail waited to bring me to my car.

A sense of panic churned in my gut as if I wouldn't see Kir again. That everything had been a dream, something I'd conjured up out of my inability to let go of the past.

A very tall Black man in a tailored suit and eyes shaded by

dark-framed sunglasses approached me. He carried himself with confidence as if he could take out anyone who dared to mess with him. He was definitely more than private security.

He had to be one of Kir's Solon contacts.

"Mrs. King. Here are your keys. Your car is refueled and your personal belongings are hidden in the concealed compartment under the passenger seat."

"Thank you." I opened my fingers, and he placed my keys with a hummingbird keyring in my palm.

As I turned to go in the direction of my car, he said, "Two more things."

I paused and waited.

"First, your itinerary is with your belongings. You will need to review it and follow it exactly as stated."

We'd see about that.

I nodded. "And the second thing?"

"Mr. Silva wants complete transparency, so he wanted you to know there are eyes on you at all times when you are out in public."

Silva. That's right. From this point on, he wasn't Kir King. He was Antoni Silva.

"I know. My security is with me."

"No, in addition to them."

I narrowed my gaze. "Is that right? Can I assume it's more of his agency favors?"

"Yes, ma'am."

"I swear, Kir, I'm going to kick your ass when I see you again," I muttered to myself.

"If it makes you feel any better," the man added, "Mr. Silva is under the same protocol."

"Well, there is that." I moved in the direction of my car.

Kir's need to protect me had no bounds.

I opened my door and slid into the driver's seat of my Mercedes, taking a deep breath to center myself. That was when the scent of my perfume inside the car hit me.

I looked around me.

This was impossible. Everything looked as it had days ago.

This couldn't be the same car.

I pressed buttons on the console to see if my preferred setting was in place and opened all the compartments. Nothing was out of place.

Suddenly, I remembered something Danika had told me when we'd worked on some of our projects for Solon.

Once you become one of them, they will have your back whenever and wherever you need them. No job was too small or too impossible.

I'd never officially worked for them, only helping with projects assigned to Danika. Kir, on the other hand, was an insider, and they'd mobilized for him.

Well, I guessed I couldn't be mad at someone having his back, especially since I had Sylvia and all her resources. Resources I was utilizing for a project I didn't need anyone finding out about until it was in motion. I'd have to make a few calls once I was positive no one could track me.

Pushing those thoughts back, I pressed the button to turn on the car engine, set my GPS to the Miami Ladai Room, and began my journey.

How the fuck was I going to pretend everything was the same when everything was different?

I was no longer the grieving widow. I had a living, breathing husband. A man I'd spent the last two days with. A man I had to pretend was another man.

And then there was Luke. What the fuck was I going to tell him?

It wasn't right to give him any hope. I'd have to call him. First, I'd apologize for standing him up last night and then tell him there was no chance of us being more than friends.

I shouldn't have accepted the date in the first place. Any relationship with me would have a finite ending going in. Now with Kir in the mix, I had to adjust everything in my life.

Damn, my list of things to do kept getting longer and longer. Good thing I could multitask. But that would have to wait until I was sure my husband and his team of spies hadn't bugged my car.

For now, I'd listen to the latest audiobook from one of my favorite romance novelists, focus on the road, and deal with the crazy Miami drivers.

AN HOUR LATER, I ARRIVED OUTSIDE THE GIANT WHITE nondescript building that housed the Ladai Room. In the light of day, the club looked like every other building just outside the Coconut Grove section of Miami, or, as the locals called it, "The Grove." It was an up-and-coming area, ready for redevelopment with prime real estate for anyone willing to take the time to invest.

Right now, no one from the outside would believe this office building housed twenty small boxing arenas as well as one main event space. Then again, it was mid-morning and only those who worked in the buildings around here would venture to these parts.

But come tonight, everything would change. An aura of danger and darkness would descend on the place. It was more of a trick to the senses that I learned from my nightclubs. The correct lighting and scents could do wonders to set the mood for a place.

In addition to the change in look, the Ladai Room security would canvas the property, only allowing those with paid membership inside with no exception—no drivers, no personal bodyguards, no weapons, no electronics. The only guests allowed were those preapproved and thoroughly background-checked. Anyone caught attempting to break the rules was permanently banned from both of the Ladai Room locations.

I pulled through the large access gate of the property and couldn't help but smile.

I'd gotten such a bargain for the place and all thanks to Sam.

When I'd come up with my concept for the clubs, I'd enlisted Sam's help to scout out locations. He may not have gotten to play big brother to me while growing up, but he'd stepped in when I needed him. He'd homed in on this particular location as perfect for what I wanted. It had space, privacy, and ambiance.

I slowed the car and frowned, gripping the steering wheel a little tighter.

Sam was another person to add to my list of people whose ass I needed to kick. He'd known about Kir and kept it from me. He was my damn brother. He was supposed to have my back.

Well, shit. Sam was technically Kir's brother too.

I couldn't help but growl inside.

Fucking Kings.

I released a deep breath, accepting there was nothing I could do about any of the Kings at the moment.

As I drove toward the back of the building, I noticed fencing going up between some of the older buildings. It was a good indication that renovations of some type were about to start. Whatever it was, the more urban feel of the construction site would add to the edge I gave with my lighting and decor.

The clients I drew into the Ladai Room had deep pockets and needed the illusion of grit without the actual danger of the streets.

Pulling into the garage under the building, I waited for my team to clear me and then parked in my designated spot.

I'd always had strict security, even if the events over the last few days may have made it seem as if I was walking around with my head in the clouds.

After my stabbing, I'd never taken my safety for granted. I'd lost too much and refused to let anyone take anything from me again.

That was something else Kir and I had to address. Eventually. When I was ready.

I still held a pang of resentment for having to go through the pain of holding our little girl's lifeless body in my arms and then having to bury her without the knowledge that I wasn't alone.

A lump formed in my throat. No. I shook my head. I wouldn't go there. This was not the time or the place for those emotions. I'd worked too hard to push those feelings down.

One day Kir and I would have to face them.

First, we had a shitload of other things to wade through.

Stepping out of the car, I made my way to what looked like an emergency call box. I pressed my thumb to the side of it, and it opened up like a cabinet. Inside sat a series of various electronics I used when working on projects for Danika. I picked out an encrypted cellphone and closed the cabinet.

No one could track this bad boy. Well, maybe Danika, but it would take her a minute or two. It was a product developed by one of Sylvia's companies and used by her organization.

I turned on the phone and then dialed Lilly Lennox's number.

Yes, she was Danika's new assistant at her New York gallery, but technically Lilly had been my friend before Danika even met her. Lilly was another of Sylvia's rescues. We'd met while I was in Greece and bonded. Lilly understood what it was like to have your world shatter and then stumble around to rebuild it.

"Jay, thank God. You had us worried," Lilly said with an accent that was more British than German. "How are you handling everything?"

I leaned against the garage wall. "As well as can be expected. Make sure you call Sylvia and give her an update. I don't want her causing more issues if she finds out anything about this."

"Already handled."

"Any updates on the tracing?"

"Dani is still working on it. Right now, she is following a loop of servers around the world to whoever these assholes hired to place the hit in the first place. She is more interested in nailing the bastards who took the job than who ordered it."

"You and I already know who ordered it."

"We know, but Dani doesn't. She has no idea what you did to force his hand. Are you going to tell Dani what we did?"

"No." I released a deep breath. "This isn't her fight. It's mine."

"But she's my boss now. And she's your cousin."

"You have more than one boss. Dani just happens to be one of them."

"She could help us."

"She can't know any of this. She'll try to stop me. Dani thinks she's the only one allowed to take risks. She has her way of handling Papa. I'm creating my own way. I will never be his victim again."

"We made this plan before you found out Kir was alive. I don't want you to do this anymore. The ends don't justify the means."

I closed my eyes for a second. "We're going to alter the plan but not stop it."

"Jay, please."

"We still have to look out for my mom. And it's not going to bring my little girl back. Besides, Papa shouldn't do illegal things if he doesn't want them to bite him in the ass."

"What we are doing could be considered questionable."

"Yeah well, questionable is par for the course in our world. And for the record, on paper, everything we have done is legal."

"If that is how you want to look at it. I'll go with that line of thought."

"Lilly, answer this question."

"Go ahead."

I thought for a second and knew I had to ask. "Did you know about Kir?"

"No," she exclaimed. "I found out when Dani stormed into

my office and said Kir had you and we needed to find the people who put contracts on your abduction. The brothers are always poking around the gallery and never revealed anything."

"I believe you. All of this is a bit overwhelming."

"I get it." Lilly was quiet for a few moments. "If I get fired for helping you, you better give me a job in one of your clubs."

"You're an heiress. You don't need money."

"I won't touch that money or give my parents hope of my coming back. I've done enough to damage to the family. It's better that I stay away."

The pain I always heard in her voice whenever she talked about the aftermath of her relationship made me want to put a bullet through her ex's head. Thankfully, someone had already taken care of it.

"You know as well as I do that it wasn't your fault. He used you."

"Because of me, my best friend nearly died and my father has to deal with people questioning his loyalty. I brought that bastard into our lives."

"And I brought Papa into Kir's."

"Speaking of Kir. Are you going to tell him?"

"He hasn't earned my secrets."

"And if he finds out? The brothers are nosey as hell, especially Rey. That man thinks he has a right to information just because he's curious. Asshole." The animosity she had against Rey made me want to laugh.

From the moment the two of them had met, there was a mutual dislike. They couldn't be in the same room without irritating one another. Danika and I liked to joke that it was foreplay, but the idea of the two of them together was a little scary. If that happened, I had no doubt blood would spill.

"I will address the Kir situation if it arises. All you need to worry about is making sure the funds I transferred remain hidden. Once that happens, there isn't a thing anyone can do. Papa will never be able to hurt Mummy again, and he will have to find another way to fund his campaign."

"This is a dangerous game you're playing."

"He's already tried to have me abducted. And with the changes I'm making to our plan, I'm more valuable to him healthy and alive than dead. Dead, everything I own goes to the Kings. And the last thing Ashok Shah wants to happen is to have any of Shah's assets go to the Kings."

"Jay, let me tell Dani. I promise she won't stop us. She's better at this shit than any of us."

"We'll bring her in when we have no choice."

"You're still mad that she knew about Kir."

"Maybe. I'm not sure. It just hurts to know that so many people kept him from me."

"She's on our side. But I get it. You know with Kir back, your father's hopes of forcing you to marry the right boy are squashed."

"First of all, no one can force me to do shit. And second, Kir isn't back. He's Antoni Silva."

"I want to ask you one more time to bring Dani in on this. She has resources we don't. Hell, she *is* the resource."

"Fine, tell her. Then have her call me. I'm sure I'm going to get an ass-chewing."

Lilly released a relieved breath. "You mean after she gives me one?"

"One for all and all for one and all that shit."

"You're such an asshole. And for the record, that's not the saying."

I couldn't help but smirk as I glanced at my watch. "I need to go. Make sure to clear the log on this conversation."

"I know my job. Don't get abducted again."

"I'll do my best not to." I ended the call and slipped the phone into my handbag before making my way toward the staff entrance to the building.

A quick press of my thumb against the scanner and the doors opened. I had barely turned the corner to my office when I saw Dillon coming toward me, looking annoyed and ready to strangle someone.

"Jay. I'm so glad you're here. The phone has been ringing off the hook."

I studied him for a second.

He was similar in build and height to Kir, but that was where the similarities ended. Dillon had inherited the Silva green eyes and olive skin tone whereas Kir had gotten his breathtaking dark good looks from his Indian mother.

Dillon was someone I trusted. He was the youngest of *Tia* Martha's seven children and the only one who hadn't chosen to go into the business she'd created. Dillon had gone the route of professional mixed martial arts, becoming a champion known internationally for his skills. It wasn't until a shoulder injury that he'd decided to retire.

Around the same time, I'd decided I wanted to open my clubs and called him to see if he wanted to join forces with me, and the rest was history. Dillon and I worked well together—it was more of a big-sister, younger-brother relationship.

"What's going on?"

Dillon handed me a clipboard with a list of names and messages. As I scanned them, I frowned. "This can't be right. Why would they call us? We are a private club. Not a place for a professional match, even if they are members."

Two professional boxers were requesting the main ring at the Ladai Room to settle a disagreement. The purse was in the eight figures, and the fighters expected me to hold it until the end of the match, with a percentage going to us once the refs called the fight.

"I told them. But they insisted this would be an invitation-only event for private clientele. They don't plan to advertise it. It has something to do with a girl."

I rolled my eyes. "This is not the place to have a boxing match over a girlfriend."

"I actually think it has to do with getting permission to marry the sister."

I blew out a breath. "Dillon, I haven't even made it to my office to handle this. Let me have a cup of coffee first."

"Well, I'm not the one who decided to take a few impromptu days off."

So that was what Danika had told everyone. No one would think twice about it since I'd just finished a ninety-hour week and needed to catch up on sleep.

"Whatever." I walked into the main arena area of the club.

Currently, the space setup was in a cage-like fashion, with the center ring surrounded by metal fencing. It was the standard look for MMA matches. Around the outside of the ring was stadium-style seating. The room could easily fit a thousand people, but we never let capacity get beyond five hundred.

The only members allowed to compete in that ring had to have won other minor matches and had to have physicals by our chosen physician stating they were healthy to fight. The one thing I would not risk was the welfare of my elite clientele. Many of them thought they were cream-of-the-crop athletes, but in fact, they were mediocre, at best.

The real athletes who used my facilities never ever showed their faces in public. Low profile was the name of the game for them. They used the private section of the building, one with designated security and access. I provided private training facilities with all of the state-of-the-art equipment needed without the cost to the athlete. This other aspect of my business allowed me a quick way to convert my operation if I ever tired of dealing with the assholes who couldn't get over the fact I was a woman running a club like mine.

Fucking misogynistic bullshit.

"Are you okay, Jay? You seem agitated." Dillon drew my attention back to him.

"I'm fine. I just had a few eventful days." I adjusted my shoulder bag and tucked my hair behind my ear.

Dillon set a hand on my arm, causing me to pause my steps. He narrowed his gaze, cocking his head to the side, and then a scowl formed on his face.

"Is that a bruise on the side of your face? Who the fuck hit you?"

Shit, I'd forgotten the makeup hadn't covered it up completely.

The rage on Dillon's face was something I'd never seen before and almost reminded me of his cousin.

I exhaled. Kir had warned me I'd have to let Dillon in on the plan. I thought I'd at least get to have a cup of coffee first.

Well, I guessed this was as good a time as any. "Let's go into my office. I have something to tell you and then you need to make it across town for a meeting at your mom's warehouse."

"What the fuck have you gotten into, Jay?"

"A lot, as usual. But even this story is something you're not going to believe when you hear the whole of it."

12

KIRAN

Two hours after Jayna left the island, I worked my speedboat around the Port of Miami on my way to the dock where Rey was waiting to take me to meet my *Tia* Martha and all of my paternal family. I could almost see the shock, hurt, and anger that would flash over *Tia* Martha's face before she walked up to me, smacked me, and then wrapped me in her arms as she cried.

She was the closest person I had to a mother, and I knew I'd let her down too.

I'd let a lot of people down.

Not anymore. I would fix the mess I'd made and make sure no one, not Hector, not Ashok Shah, not anyone would fuck with someone I loved again.

The ruse of Antoni Silva would only last so long. Hopefully, long enough to spring my traps and keep the most precious thing to me in the world safe.

Jayna wanted me to see the woman she was now. What she didn't realize was that I'd always seen her.

She was still the same Jayna of years ago, but now she saw in herself the woman I'd seen from the beginning. The strength and resilience were always there. She wouldn't have survived her childhood otherwise.

I gripped the back of my neck and inhaled the salty sea air.

The sex had filled a physical need and pointed a glaring spotlight on the giant void between us. Maybe by the end of this, Jayna could forgive me for the stupidity of the last few years.

As I pulled up to the dock, I saw the familiar figure of my brother, Sam, waiting for me. I guessed plans had changed in the last hour.

"So, you've decided to join the world of the living," Sam said as I threw a rope up to him and let him tie off the boat.

I jumped onto the pier. "Looks that way."

Using my hand to shield my eyes from the glare of the sun, I looked at Sam. He wore tailored slacks and a button-down shirt rolled up at the sleeves. A trail of sweat ran down the side of his face, completely clashing with his *GQ* vibe.

I wanted to ask him if the Miami heat was too much for him but kept it to myself.

"For good, or are you going into the shadows again?"

"No more shadows."

"I'm talking about after this charade."

"So am I."

"About fucking time. We need you to knock some heads together and keep people in line." Sam pulled me into a hug and then just as quickly turned, walking toward the parking lot. "Come on. I have to give you a briefing."

I shook my head. That was Sam. Little time for emotions. All business.

We considered him the youngest of the four King brothers, even though there was barely a year and a half gap between all of us. With Nik being the oldest, then me, followed by Rey and Sam.

Sam headed up what we called the public and legitimate aspects of King Holdings. He had a head for real estate and development that boggled the mind. He had a way of finding the shittiest property anywhere and turning it into a goldmine. He also had a knack for playing the market, making it easy for all of us to hand him our portfolios and watch our investments grow to insane levels.

"I thought Rey was coming."

"He got called in on an assignment."

I nodded.

Rey was the information collector of the brothers. There was nothing he or his contacts couldn't find on someone. In addition to his hacker skills, he happened to be CIA. Just like Sam, Rey was smart, and because of that, Arin had decided it was better to push for the younger two King boys to pursue college. For Rey, that also included recruitment into the CIA, and for Sam, it was business school.

We approached a black Porsche 918 Spyder.

I studied the nearly million-dollar car. This was a little over-the-top for an inconspicuous pickup.

"Whose car is this?"

"Antoni Silva's," he answered, opening the driver's door.

"Then shouldn't I be the one driving?"

"Probably, but first, we need to clear the air on a few things. Get in."

Getting in on the passenger side, I waited for Sam to speak.

When he remained too quiet for my liking, I said, "Let me hear whatever is on your mind so we can get on to business."

"I'm going to give you this one warning." Sam turned his head, holding my gaze. "If you fuck with my sister's emotions ever again, I will finish what the wreck didn't."

The determination in his eyes wasn't something I'd ever seen outside of when he went after an asset Shah was planning to purchase.

Sam and I were brothers in all things but blood. We'd shared a life on the streets of a dirty New York City neighborhood that no kid should have roamed and had survived more hardships together than young boys ever should have seen, so I knew this wasn't about us.

This was about his loyalty to a sister he hadn't been able to protect when she was younger—a sister he had to lie to for years because of me.

Sam was the son of the woman Ashok Shah seduced and pretended to love until Monica Shah's family and money came along. He'd seduced the young nineteen-year-old and left her pregnant, never looking back or thinking of the boy he'd thrown away.

"I hear what you're saying," I said.

"I mean it. Jayna has been through enough."

"I'm not going to fuck it up." At least I hoped I wouldn't.

"Make sure you don't."

"Now that we have that clear, what's the update?"

"I've told *Tia* Martha to gather everyone at the warehouse. They think we are meeting about some properties she wanted me to look over." He cupped the back of his head. "I swear, if she smacks me, I'm going to punch you in return. That woman's hand hurts."

I couldn't help but laugh. *Tia* Martha was definitely a battle-ax. But then again, she'd had no choice but to become one. As the eldest of the siblings, when she'd come over with my father and their sister, she'd gone to work in a pastry factory, working double shifts and forgoing her personal dreams. Eventually, she'd decided to start a small bakery with her savings, and over the years, she'd expanded to multiple locations all over Miami. Through her efforts, countless members of our extended family had employment, and their children had gone to college.

When we'd connected, I'd invested in her bakeries and made sure her small enterprise expanded nationally. I had no doubt that she would have been the one to adopt me after my parents' deaths if I hadn't fallen through the cracks of the foster care system and ended up on the streets.

"I'm the one she's going to smack. First, she'll get all weepy, and then she'll wallop me on the back of the head."

"You deserve it."

"I know." I looked out the window. "Do you think she'll go along with the plan?"

"She won't like it. The last thing she wants to do is tie herself to anything to do with Victor Silva."

"Without her getting the word out, this isn't going to work."

"She'll give you hell, but you know she's going to do it." Sam leaned down and opened a compartment hidden under the seat, pulling out a folder. "Here."

"What is it?"

"Everything for you to become Antoni Silva, real estate mogul, mixed martial artist, and partner in the Ladai Room. For the next few weeks, you need to follow the itinerary Danika set up and make appearances in those exact places at those exact times."

I flipped through the details. I couldn't believe how thorough everything was.

"Was this created by Danika or Devani?"

Devani Patel was an NYC socialite with whom Sam had an on-again, off-again friends-with-benefits type relationship. She was also a member of Solon. In fact, she was the one who'd recruited me, but those were secrets I wasn't allowed to share even with my brothers. So, needless to say, I was surprised to learn Sam and Devani were hooking up after a poker game two years ago.

"Does it matter?"

"I guess not."

"Then why are we talking about it?"

I wanted to smirk at the irritation in his voice. It was almost too easy to get under his skin when it came to Devani. She was the one person Sam couldn't string along. It was more like she strung him along, and it pissed him off to have the tables turned on him.

I flipped to the last page of the schedule. "Six weeks?"

"You already knew it could take that long. Why are you surprised? Besides, you were apart for nearly three years. A few more weeks shouldn't be a big deal."

There was no point in trying to explain it. Now that I was back in Jayna's life, truly back, the thought of what I'd done seemed like the stupidest decision I had ever made.

In a matter of hours, she'd accepted my truth and me, accepted my plan, accepted this was how it was going to have to be for us to find a way back together.

I would not fuck this up a second time.

"Make sure you keep her in the loop."

"She'll find out. Danika sent her a similar packet." Sam studied me for a second. "Did she knock you on your ass or something? You're the guy who lives in the shadows. Now you're ready to draw the attention of anyone who dares to look in her direction. Hell, you're about to antagonize all the players to come after you."

I remembered how Jayna flipped me onto my back and stalked into the house, and almost smiled.

"You could say it was something like that. The first time round, Jayna chased me. This time, I'm the one who has to do the chasing and hope she decides to keep me."

The car pulled up to a collection of warehouses labeled with the name *Martha's Bakeries and Distribution*. Once we passed through security, I took a deep breath and prepared myself to face the only other woman outside of Jayna who I loved unconditionally.

"Calm down, asshole. You look as if you're going to puke. If you survived Jayna, I'm sure little *Tia* Martha will be a piece of cake."

I shot Sam a death glare and said, "Don't make me punch you."

"As Nik says, we all have to pay the piper eventually." Sam opened his door. "Let's go. They're waiting."

13

JAYNA

Two weeks after returning to my normal life—well, life as normal as Jayna King's life could be—I arrived at Cameli, a Michelin-starred restaurant hidden inside one of Luke's hotels on South Beach.

I was overdue for a lunch with Luke, and after going back and forth with our busy work schedules, we'd finally set today as the day to meet.

I felt I had to explain in more detail why I'd stood him up for our date. He'd accepted the text I'd sent saying I'd had an emergency meeting with a business partner, but I still felt terrible about how it had all turned out.

Blowing someone off wasn't my style.

Strike that, with the exception of Ashok Shah.

I'd made blowing him off an art form. Even before Kir had

disappeared from my life, no one could convince me to do something I was adamantly against without a solid reason.

I sighed as I approached the hostess. I only hoped by the end of this lunch, Luke and I were friends.

He was a nice guy—overbearing at times, but a nice guy.

"May I help you?" the hostess with long blond hair, bright green eyes, and a warm smile asked.

"Yes, I believe Mr. Joshi is waiting for me."

She gestured to her right. "Come this way. He told me to bring you back."

As I followed her, I felt a slight prickle of awareness down my spine.

Kir.

He wasn't supposed to be here.

I scanned the diners, not seeing anyone familiar.

Releasing a deep breath, I focused ahead of me. It was just my mind playing tricks.

I'd gone almost three years without the man, and now two weeks without him seemed unbearable. Even when he was back in the city, we wouldn't have the same relationship.

He'd come back as Antoni Silva, not Kir.

Through the briefings Danika sent me, I learned Antoni had made appearances in Vegas, LA, and New York. He'd bought large chunks of real estate from port space to luxury development spaces.

There had to be a reason he was buying all of those properties. I'd have to ask Sam—he'd know.

Well, that would require communication with him, and for now, the only King I'd spoken to was Danika. I was still too hurt.

Then again, if I stayed out of the King/Silva business, Kir wouldn't need to poke his nose into mine.

After Lilly had relayed my plan to Danika and I'd had my expected ass-chewing, Danika had jumped in headfirst, ready to make sure there was an extra layer of protection between what I was implementing and Papa.

I wouldn't lie to myself and say it wasn't a relief to have the resources of a Dark Web hacker at my back. Now Mummy's money was safe from Papa, and the very companies Papa illegally put in my name and tried to pass to Arun Joshi through a forced marriage were part of a trust based out of Switzerland.

As I turned a corner and saw Luke sitting against the back corner of the restaurant, I pushed down all thoughts of Papa.

Luke rose as I came into view, a big grin on his face. He was dressed in his usual stylish suit that made him look as if he'd stepped out of the pages of a fashion magazine.

There was no doubt he was a handsome man.

And I felt nothing. No tingle. No spark. No anything.

It was all because of the unpolished street kid turned possessive man who was determined to protect me whether I liked it or not.

As I neared, Luke took my hand and said, "You stood me up."

"I can explain," I responded.

He drew me close to him for a kiss.

I thought he was going for my cheek when I realized he was heading for my lips and turned my face. He grazed my cheek, and I almost sighed in relief.

Pulling back, I ignored his frown and slipped into my chair.

A waiter came up to our table, filling the water and taking my drink order before leaving again.

"So, who is this business partner? Do I know him?"

"Probably not. He likes to keep a low profile."

"Is he invested in the dance clubs or the Ladai Room locations?"

I narrowed my gaze. "Does it matter? We just had to get a few things settled."

"And are they settled?"

"For the most part. As with any partnership, there are ups and downs."

"Why did you need an investor if you have your inheritance and the King portfolio?"

"What's with the twenty questions? I know my business. You know yours. Tell me, why did you take on investors in your hotels when you can finance your own projects?"

A flash of irritation crossed his face before he schooled it away. "Point made. I just worry about you."

This was the first time he'd ever wanted to know so much about my business. Hell, I'd offered to show him my clubs several times over the last months, and he'd declined, and now he wanted to know why I'd taken on a partner.

I pushed down my annoyance, realizing he thought I ditched him for a meeting with my partner.

"You don't need to worry. I've got it under control." Picking up my glass, I took a sip of my water.

"Leaning on other people isn't a weakness, you know? I have a lot of experience when it comes to dealing with partners and business."

Where the hell had that come from?

Inhaling deeply to calm myself, I said in the most direct tone I could manage, "Luke, as I've already stated, I've got it under control. I appreciate what you are trying to say, but you know nothing about the industries behind either of my businesses. If I were having a problem, I would consult with the advisers I already have in place."

"Okay. Okay." He lifted his hands in surrender. "I hear you. Let's drop the subject."

His gesture said he was ready to move on, but the rigid set of his face told me he wasn't happy with my response.

"What else is bothering you? This has got to be about more than just our missed date."

He shook his head. "I apologize. I had a hard morning and brought my foul mood with me."

"Want to share?"

"Let's say it has to do with the same types of issues we share with our fathers."

Immediately all my annoyance from moments ago disappeared. Arun Joshi, like Papa, used his money and privilege to control his family. Luke hadn't taken the "fuck you" approach I had in handling his father. Instead, he'd tried to become the perfect son, doing everything and anything his father expected.

That was until his fiancée Seema's death. Then something in him snapped, and he'd decided to put a respectable distance between himself and his father, letting his younger brother step in to become the heir apparent.

He'd rebelled in his way, and I respected him for it. I understood how hard it was to fight against the constraints of the society we'd grown up in.

"I've dumped enough of my issues with Papa on you. You can always tell me."

He opened his mouth to respond, but at that moment, the server returned with our drinks and took our order.

Once we were alone again, I said, "Well, go on."

He drank down half his cocktail before he answered, "It's nothing more than him telling me to do my duty and to stop playing around and get the job done by the family."

"Meaning, get married, have a few kids, and fall into line with the plans your father set for you."

"Exactly." His gaze went to my left hand as it rested on the table. "Can I ask you a question?"

I had a feeling I knew what he wanted to know.

"Go ahead." I lifted the glass of wine to my lips for a sip.

"Does any man have a real chance with you outside of Kiran King's reincarnation?"

I coughed, nearly choking on my wine and covering my mouth not to spit the liquid all over the table.

"W-what makes you ask that?"

"You still haven't taken those rings off. I'm not sure you ever will."

I thought of the way Kir had watched me as I left the island, the love and determination in his eyes.

He was a man who'd always lived behind the scenes. He never liked big events or parties. He was more comfortable in smaller groups and using his fists in the ring.

For us, he was going to become someone public, someone who would draw a lot of attention.

I looked up at Luke's face. "I'm not sure what answer you

want me to give. The rings represent my past, present, and future. It's hard to imagine a future without him in it."

"Then I guess you and I will always remain in the friend zone."

I almost sighed in relief. Luke was giving me the opening I needed.

"I don't want to give you false hope. I shouldn't have agreed to the date. I apologize."

"Don't apologize. What you had with King was different. It's hard for anyone to compete with that. Now I won't lie and say that I'm not disappointed. But I do understand."

"You're a good friend, Luke." I set my hand over his and squeezed.

"Friends it is."

After our food arrived, we ate, and we fell into some fun discussions about a variety of topics, from movies and shows to the latest updates on our friends back in New York.

Just as I was about to leave at the end of our lunch, Luke gave me a smile that reminded me of the Luke from our younger years when he wanted something and said, "So since we're friends and all…"

"Yes."

"Remember when you invited me to take a peek inside the Ladai Room?"

"Yep. I also remember you telling me boxing and MMA weren't your things."

"I decided to be more open-minded and see it from your perspective. That is if you are still willing to show me."

I hesitated for a split second, wondering how this would

look to Kir, but then remembered I was friends with Luke, nothing more. If Kir had issues, then he'd have to get over them.

"Of course. I'm proud of what I've created. Send me a message with a few dates that work for you, and I'll look at our schedule. As long as we don't have any private events in the main arena, I'll clear you to come."

The valet attendant arrived with my car and opened the door.

"It's a date." He leaned in, kissing my cheek.

"As friends," I reminded him as I slid into my seat.

"Yes, I know. As friends."

Just as the door was closing, I saw the silhouette of a man I knew was no longer a ghost.

He stood in the shadows of a distant hotel. The number of people strolling down the sidewalk helped disguise him, but I had no doubt it was him.

My heartbeat accelerated.

I knew I didn't just imagine the feeling.

He wasn't supposed to be in Miami for at least another few weeks.

I could almost feel the weight of his gaze on me.

Oh well. He would deal.

The car in front of me moved, and I had no choice but to move too. Shifting my car in drive, I pulled out of the driveway and onto the road, in the opposite direction of the man scowling at me.

14

KIRAN

I walked up to the Miami headquarters of Martin Imports, feeling the urge to punch something. It had taken every bit of my control not to march over to the hotel Joshi owned and keep myself from grabbing Jayna, throwing her over my shoulder, and making damn sure everyone knew she was mine.

Yeah. It was completely insane and a tad barbaric, but that fucker had his hands on my woman.

"Where the hell have you been?" Joel, my head of security, came toward me in as much rage as I felt inside.

Joel was a tall Black man who towered over my six-two frame by at least six inches. He was built like a tank, solid in a reinforced-brick-wall way. He was also a Solon agent with fifteen years of training under his belt.

We'd sparred plenty of times, and I'd won as many rounds as

I'd lost. Where he had the brawn, I was fast and had the element of surprise. He was also one of the few people outside of my brothers who'd kept me connected to the outside world over the last few years. In fact, he was the one who'd pushed me into seeing a psychiatrist. He'd dealt with his share of shit on the job and knew it would help me.

Right now, the look on his face said he was ready to give me a beat-down.

I probably shouldn't have slipped my detail. My only excuse was it was stifling, and I wasn't used to it anymore. The thought of anyone knowing my every move annoyed the fuck out of me.

Then my dumbass self decided to check up on Jayna.

How the hell had she known I was there?

"I had to take care of something."

"How do you expect us to watch your back if you keep slipping out like that? Dammit. You know better."

"I know. I know."

"How'd she look?"

Of course, he'd known I'd gone to see Jayna. Joel had been the one who'd delivered Jayna's Mercedes to her two weeks ago.

"Good." I almost smirked. "She saw me."

"Getting rusty?" Joel fell into step with me as we approached the glass doors of the building.

"Looks that way."

He pulled open the doors, and we moved toward the elevators. "Maybe you should retire."

"My old job opened up, so that's a possibility." I checked my watch. "Everyone in position?"

"The team is already inside."

I nodded. "Do you have the contracts?"

"Yes. Everything is upstairs. Are you ready to play your role?"

"You mean an asshole?" We stepped into the open cab of an elevator. "I was born one according to my brothers, so it shouldn't be a problem. Besides, this is what I've done since I was a fucking teenager. I'm just doing it under a different name."

"That's right—the King enforcer. I forgot. I've only seen you do the negotiation thing."

The last assignment Joel and I'd worked on involved brokering the sale of conflict diamonds as a way to infiltrate a human trafficking ring. I'd made the introductions and positioned Joel as the seller of the diamonds. In the end, my role assisted in the rescue of four hundred men, women, and children from an unspeakable existence.

"It's not as dramatic as you believe. Well, not to me anyway. It's more about scaring the asshole who reneged on a deal. I've rarely, if ever, had to get my hands truly dirty."

As the King enforcer, I was supposed to put the fear of God into someone without actually hurting anyone. Under Arin's training, I'd learned that the threat of potential harm was as effective as carrying out the act. Especially with the Wall Street and political types. The possibility of ruining their finances or public reputations had them paying up on the favors they'd bartered with us.

"Don't kill anyone. I don't have time to clean up the mess."

"The minute one of them starts sniffling, you'll be the one cocking the gun in their direction."

"Probably." The elevator doors opened.

We stepped out onto the executive floor of Martin Imports, where an older Latina woman who looked to be in her fifties sat behind a large reception desk. The rest of the floor was empty except for her.

We'd planned this meeting on a day where the staff was at a team-building retreat. A retreat the executive of the company didn't feel was important enough to attend.

The woman's eyes widened as she took in my appearance. I wasn't sure if I'd ever get used to that initial reaction most people had after seeing my scars.

Once she regained her composure, she said, "Hello. May I help you?"

"Yes, Silva. I have an appointment with Mr. Martin."

"One moment." She looked at her computer monitor. "Let me notify him you arrived early."

At that moment, my team slipped onto the floor through the stairwell. I gestured with a nod, and they moved in the direction of the owner and CEO's office.

"No need to call him. We'll head back and start our meeting sooner rather than later." Joel and I moved around the desk and strode toward the closed door.

"B-but," she stuttered and then gasped as she noticed the group of men and women waiting for us.

She must have moved since I heard someone say, "I wouldn't do that. I suggest you stay right there until we leave."

Joel opened the door, and both Jonathan Martin Senior and Junior froze. They looked as if they were packing up for the day. Interesting.

"Going somewhere?" I walked in, my crew following behind me and lining the walls of the room.

Fear entered Martin Junior's eyes, and without a doubt, I knew his father had no idea what baby boy had done with his family's assets.

Good thing for me, Junior's double-cross played right into today's plan.

"As a matter of fact, we were," Senior said, his annoyance apparent in his curt response and the standoffish glare he shot at me. "Who are you?"

My respect for the man grew. He was no pushover.

"Your three o'clock appointment."

"I don't have anything on my calendar. In fact, I would be with my team at their retreat if I didn't have a damn doctor's appointment to go to."

I liked the man more and more. It was Junior who was the asshole of the two, who couldn't mix with the worker bees.

"But Junior here does." I stared Martin Junior in the eyes.

He shifted his gaze away as sweat dotted his face.

A week ago, Nik had sent a message to Martin, notifying him all debts were due by three p.m. today. Martin was well aware if he didn't deliver, someone would come to collect.

In reality, we knew he'd never have the means to fulfill his end of the bargain. He'd overextended himself with risky ventures and promised too many people the same things he'd used as leverage with us.

"Jon, what is he talking about?"

Joel moved in Senior's direction and guided him to a chair. At the same time, another team member grabbed Junior by the back of the neck and brought him over to me.

"Would you like to tell him, or should I do the honors?" I asked.

Junior started whimpering as he noticed the holster inside my suit jacket.

Joel rolled his eyes, and I almost smirked, knowing he was ready to punch the man for being such a wimp.

"I guess the honor is mine. Tell me, Mr. Martin—" I turned my back to Junior and strolled toward Senior, "—what do you know of the King brothers?"

"You didn't. Why didn't you come to me first?" Senior looked around me toward his son.

"I...I didn't have a choice. It was the only way I could get the project completed on time and under cost."

I thought of Jayna and all the choices I was making so our lives would connect again.

"We always have a choice. You just got greedy. Now I'm here to collect on your deal," I said.

"What was the deal?" Martin Senior pulled a handkerchief from his pocket and dabbed his face.

Fuck. I hoped the old man wasn't going to have a heart attack on us.

As if sensing my same thoughts, Stephanie, one of the agents on the team who was a trained physician, shifted to stand next to him.

"Your son asked for the Kings' assistance with the construction and successful launch of your Las Vegas convention retail center. Your son was supposed to provide storage containers and access to your ships for one of the King mineral subsidiaries in exchange. Neither of which happened."

"We sold that part of the business months ago to purchase the port and the cargo warehouses for the new division." Martin Senior's voice filled with disbelief.

And there was the reason for today's visit. We'd known Junior had sold the long-haul shipping side of the business but were holding on to this knowledge until it was convenient for something we needed.

It turned out the warehouse and port were what we needed.

Controlling the ports meant I, Antoni Silva, had the means and the access to import and export the product I supposedly sold in and out of the United States.

Having as solid a cover as possible was the key to making sure Hector Estefan and I had a face-to-face.

"We know. And therefore, what you purchased is forfeited to me."

"You mean to the Kings," Junior said.

"No, to me. I purchased the favors you owed the Kings from them."

"What do you mean, you purchased the favors? That's not how it works."

"That's exactly how it works when you don't pay up."

"Who are you?"

"I'm Antoni Silva."

Real fear entered his eyes and I almost smiled. I guessed the rumors everyone was spreading about me had reached Junior's ears.

"But you can call me the debt collector."

On cue, a folder and pen were set in front of both men.

I glanced to my side. "On that table is a contract. Sign it."

"What?" Junior said as if not comprehending my words.

"You sold something that wasn't yours to sell and then purchased a high-value commodity with the proceeds. Now it belongs to me."

"I'm not signing anything. I didn't make a deal for the ships or the company."

"That's where you're wrong. When you go back on your word, the debt collector sets the price."

"You can't be serious about the cargo dock. I…I…it's…I have contracts on the space. I have to honor them."

"What happened to honoring your agreement with Kings?" I fisted Junior's hair and pulled him forward. "Sign."

I held him over the table as he clawed at my hands. It was at that moment I realized how young Junior was. He couldn't be more than in his mid-twenties, if that.

Dumb fuck.

He should know better than to deal with people like my brothers and me. Especially if he knew he couldn't afford to pay up. Nik never shied away from telling anyone the consequence of not following through. Everyone always had the option of walking away, no harm done, before favors were exchanged.

Idiot.

Behind us, I heard someone cock a pistol. Immediately, Junior stopped struggling.

"Jon, sign the damn thing," Martin Senior ordered in a hoarse voice. "Martins always pay our debts."

"Pops, I'm sorry," Junior said as he reached for the pen and opened the folder.

I continued to hold his hair in a tight grip as he put his signature on every place there was a sticker. When he finished, I released him, and he slumped to the floor.

"Thank you for your time."

Adjusting my suit jacket, I made my way out the door and into the executive reception area.

The receptionist watched me with wary eyes but kept quiet.

I glanced over my shoulder and found father and son in a daze. Both stared down at the copy of the papers they'd signed.

Joel and I stepped onto the waiting elevator and just as the cab doors closed, I heard, "Jon, you're fired."

I almost felt sorry for the kid.

Fuck, I was getting soft. I had to get it together.

"When this is over, are you going to give it back to the idiot?" Joel asked once we stepped out of the office building.

"Most likely. I like the old man. He didn't deserve it."

"But you're going to make the kid live in misery for a while."

"Yep. We all fuck up. I'm a prime example. Junior is just too young and needs to let his balls drop before he jumps in with the sharks."

Joel shook his head. "You Kings act all scary and have everyone believing you're the boogeymen making people pay a price for a favor. Then you say shit like that. Acting as if you care about the future of a rich overprivileged prick. It's fucking confusing as hell."

"I didn't say I cared about the kid. I said he fucked up. He needs to grow up."

"Same difference."

"You're just pissed off that you didn't get to punch him."

"He would have deserved it."

I wasn't going to deny it. Instead, I asked, "Where to next?"

"A trip to Houston. You have a meeting with Lightwheel Development. They owe the Kings a favor, one that now belongs to Antoni Silva."

As soon as he said Lightwheel Development, I couldn't help but smile. They were the hotel development group interested in partnering with Ashok Shah to expand his boutique hotel empire.

"This is going to be the highlight of my day. Let's go fuck up Ashok Shah's plans."

A LITTLE PAST MIDNIGHT, I WALKED INTO THE BEDROOM OF MY hotel room in downtown Houston after a long shower, ready for some sleep. The meeting with Lightwheel Development had gone better than anything I'd ever expected.

Even before Nik had contacted Dustan Marks, the head of the group that ran the company, to call in the favor he owned him, Marks had been ready to pull out of his negotiations with Shah and his hotels. Marks had heard rumors that Shah had overextended himself to finance some of his projects, and partnering could lead to disaster.

By the time my plane touched down at George Bush International, he was ready to work with me to expand his business.

I hated the wheeling-and-dealing aspect of business. Under the King Holdings umbrella, Nik or Sam would have taken the reins of this. And when it came to my ventures separate from my brothers, Jayna had taken the reins. But as Silva, I had to play the part.

It would all be worth it in the end.

I walked over to the floor-to-ceiling window and gazed out at the city. This place was so different from home. Here, everything seemed to grow quieter at night. In New York City, the hustle and bustle never stopped.

My phone buzzed on the table, making me frown. No one was supposed to have that number outside of Joel and my brothers, and we'd just finished our debriefing half an hour ago.

Walking over to the mobile, I picked it up and read the caller ID.

Jayna's cell number was displayed. What the hell?

I answered before the ringing stopped. "Is everything okay?"

"Yes. Everything is fine."

Relief washed over me. Then I frowned.

"How did you get this number?"

"I have my ways." The humming way she said that made me smile.

"Danika hacked Nik's phone and gave it to you."

"Nope. I don't need her help to hack a damn phone." She sounded offended. "I do know my way around a computer, Kir."

"Antoni," I corrected.

She sighed. "Right. Antoni."

"So, which of the brothers did you hack?"

"Sam. He decided to ambush me since I was avoiding his calls and showed up at my penthouse."

"Did you hand him his ass?"

"You could say that."

"Are you good now?"

"I guess. Sam is my brother. It's going to take me a bit to get over him lying to me for years. But then again, he's your brother too."

"How the hell did you get him away from his phone? He's attached to it."

"Once we settled things, I made him dinner."

"So, between the main course and dessert, you found time to break into his phone."

"It's really not that hard. Besides, I had years of training while I worked with Danika."

"You never stop surprising me, Princesa."

I waited for her to reprimand me for calling her that, but she didn't.

"Are you still in Miami?"

"No, I'm in Houston."

"Is it hot there?"

"About the same as where you are." I walked back to the window. "You know we're not supposed to have any communication for another few weeks. That was part of the plan."

"You broke the rules earlier today when you showed up at my lunch."

"How did you know it was me?"

"I just knew. Then when the sun shifted, I saw your face."

"He likes to touch you." I clenched my jaw. "I don't like it."

"We're friends. You'll have to get used to me having friends that are men. In the business I'm in, I have a lot of them."

"I don't care about the others. You didn't agree to a date with them."

"Why are you jealous?"

I thought about it for a second.

Why was I jealous?

Fuck. I knew why.

"Because he was the one you were supposed to be with. The one who was perfect for you. The one picked out for your perfect life."

"Obviously he wasn't perfect for me since I picked you."

"Have you?"

Over the last two weeks, I'd had a lot of time to think. And I'd realized, everything I was doing wasn't to clear a path to stay together but to see if Jayna and I had any future at all. If she could forgive me for the three years. And if she couldn't, I'd have to figure out how to live without her.

"Kir…Antoni. I picked you long ago. That's why…" She paused as if to gather her thoughts and then started again. "That's why I called. I wanted to talk to you, get to know you as you are now."

"You don't think we can do that when we're together?"

"We were together less than forty-eight hours and we barely kept our hands off each other. Sex isn't what we need right now."

"We were making up for lost time."

"And what excuse are you going to use when we see each other again?"

"Magnetic attraction."

"You're incorrigible." I could hear the smile in her words, bringing one to my own lips.

We were quiet for a few moments, then she asked, "Will you do it? Us talking. Us getting to know each other and how we've changed over the last few years."

I'd do anything for her. She had to know this by now.

"Yes."

She released a deep breath as if she thought I'd say no.

God, we really did need to get to know each other again.

"So, we're virtual dating for the next four weeks?"

"I guess you could call it that."

This could be fun. Jayna and I technically never dated. We'd gone from being nothing to inseparable.

"One more question." I moved to my bed, opened the covers, and then stretched out.

"What?"

"Does this mean phone sex is off the table?"

"It all depends on how interesting of a virtual date you are, Mr. Silva."

"Then I better make sure I keep you captivated, Mrs. King."

15

JAYNA

"Come this way," I said to Luke as we made our way into the Ladai Room.

Tonight was the only night since our lunch that both of our schedules worked well enough for him to visit the club. With my relenting to Dillon's request for the private event and other clients with deep pockets who wanted to hold similar gatherings, I'd had to place more restrictions on guest access to the club than usual.

"This isn't anything like I expected." Luke took in the state-of-the-art theater-style seating as well as the lounge-like atmosphere of the VIP boxes. "This is like a high-end sports club."

I narrowed my eyes. What the hell did he think my club was?

A hundred-thousand-dollar signup plus a ten grand monthly fee bought a lot of perks and required facilities to match.

"That's what this is. Why do you think boxing matches in Vegas go for such astronomical purses? This is big business."

He continued to look around, strolling toward the deck overlooking the main arena where a fight was taking place.

"Both of them look familiar. Who are they?"

I studied the pair in the ring, bobbing and weaving as they boxed. Both were a decent match and were heads of local megachurches. They had a friendly rivalry of sorts.

"That is something I can't divulge. If you know them, you know them. We don't name drop. That's the perk of the club—privacy."

"Even to me?"

"Even to you."

My answer must have annoyed him since a crease formed between his brows. What was up with him? In all the times we'd hung out together, it wasn't until recently he'd started acting this way.

Let it go, Jayna. You have enough on your mind.

Specifically, another man who wasn't happy with me at the moment. Kir and I had spoken nearly every day for the last three weeks. We'd kept it quiet, knowing Joel and Danika would probably have a cow if they found out. Technically, there was supposed to be no trace of contact between Kir and me. Since we were talking over encrypted lines, I wasn't too worried.

For the most part, the conversations I had with Kir were so easy. We never seemed to have a loss of things to discuss or more often debate since we were both very strong personalities with equally passionate opinions. And hence, the reason he wasn't happy with me.

Kir wanted to steer our conversations to topics I wasn't ready to tackle, specifically the stabbing, miscarriage, and everything that happened afterward. I, on the other hand, wanted to avoid those discussions. They brought back too many memories and too much pain.

I knew we'd have to address them sooner or later, but over the phone was not the place for that conversation to happen. Plus, there was this fear deep down that if I let everything out, we'd backtrack in all the progress we'd made. And therefore, shutting down the subject had resulted in a very pissed-off Kir.

Well, I could say Jayna and Antoni had their first official sort-of fight over the phone.

Bringing my attention back to Luke, I said, "Follow me. There's a match going on in one of the smaller arenas I think you'll enjoy."

"Now you've piqued my curiosity."

We took a hallway that led to an adjacent building and entered the training facilities of the Ladai Room.

"Holy shit. Is that—"

"Yep."

"Sparring against—"

"Yep."

In the ring were two Bollywood movie stars training for a movie where they played professional boxers. Their coach, a former Olympic gold medalist, stood off to the side, giving them instructions.

"Damn. I wish you hadn't made me put my phone in the bin. My sister would love a picture of this."

"Remember the rules. What you see here stays here."

"I know." His attention stayed focused on the happenings in the ring below us.

At that moment, Benny, one of my facility coordinators, came up to me.

"Boss, can you look over these? I wanted to make sure you're okay with the changes we had to make since Dillon got in the cage tonight."

What the hell?

"What do you mean Dillon got in the cage?"

"Umm. I assumed he cleared it with you. He said he had a beatdown to give someone and took one of the VIP rooms."

"No, he didn't mention anything during our meeting this morning." I grabbed the clipboard and scanned the names on the list. Dillon knew better than to adjust the plans.

And why the hell was he fighting on a night he was scheduled to work? I was going to kick his ass if his opponent didn't do it for me.

As I looked through the names on the room list, my heart stopped.

No way.

Street Viper versus Shadow Man?

"He wouldn't," I muttered.

"Who's Shadow Man?" Benny asked. "I've never seen him on the roster."

I knew Dillon was Street Viper. That was his nickname when he was a professional fighter, but Shadow Man? I'd only ever known one person to use that name. He'd used it since he was a teenager, joining illegal fights to make a quick buck in New York City underground clubs.

"Someone who shouldn't be here."

Kir, I swear I'm going to kick your ass too.

"Is something wrong?" Luke came up beside me.

I shook my head. "No. Why don't you keep watching the entertainment here while I take care of some things for the club?"

"I want to see you in action. Why don't you take me along with you?" Though he posed it like a request, I felt the undercurrents of an order.

I took a deep breath, pushing down my annoyance.

"Not possible. You're a guest and therefore have to stay in specific areas. I told you the rules before you got here."

"You act as if I'm going to share what I see with the public."

"If I expect my members to follow the rules, then everyone I bring into the club has to."

Why the hell was I explaining myself?

"Well, then make me a member."

"It doesn't work that way. You want to join, you have to go through the same process as everyone else."

"Is it because of your partner, Antoni Silva?"

I froze. "How do you know his name?"

"When you mentioned you were settling things with your partner, I wanted to find out as much as I could about the people you worked with in your businesses."

"Why the hell would you do that?" My temper flared.

"I was protecting you. I didn't want someone taking advantage of you."

"Let's get this straight. You had me investigated?"

"Well, it seemed as if your brothers-in-law weren't doing their job."

I resisted the urge to clench my fist and clock him. "Luke, I've succeeded all these years without you. We are friends. That is it. I brought you here because you wanted to see my club. That doesn't give you the right to poke your nose into things you know nothing about."

"Do you have any idea who the man you are in business with is? He is dangerous, and associating with him could ruin your reputation more than being a King."

He'd fucking ignored everything I just said. And what the hell did he mean by *ruin your reputation more than being a King*?

"I don't know where all of this is coming from. It looks like I need to make something clear to you. I never let my father tell me what to do, and Kir knew damn well better than to tell me what to do when it came to business. So do not expect me to let you influence me." I pressed my fingers to the bridge of my nose. "I think it's better that we call it a night."

I turned my back to him, feeling rage. Benny moved closer to me, hearing everything that had just happened.

Luke grabbed my arm, stopping me. "I'm sorry. I was out of line."

That was a fucking understatement.

"Luke, watch the match and then go home. I have a business to run."

His hold tightened. "I apologized. It won't happen again. Finish up what you need to do here and we'll go to dinner."

This was the last straw. He was just not getting it. I'd

handled overbearing men all my life. Even Kir knew when to back off. I shouldn't have agreed to this.

Luke's behavior was too damn possessive for a friend.

Did he think because I agreed to show him the club that I didn't mean what I said at lunch?

No, I wouldn't put that on my shoulders. I'd made it clear we were friends; if he thought he could change my mind, then it was on him.

Fuck that shit.

"On second thought, Benny, show Mr. Joshi out. I need to handle things in the club." I shook Luke's hand off and stalked away.

The nerve of the man.

Had I misjudged him all this time?

The last thing I wanted to do was admit that Kir had been right, but Luke was showing me a side of him I wasn't comfortable with and wouldn't tolerate.

I entered the long walkway leading to the VIP section of the club with the private match rooms and stopped at a panel. I looked up at the security cameras, nodding to whoever was assigned to monitor this hallway, and then placed my thumb on the ID pad. After it beeped green, I typed in my code and opened the doors.

Yeah, my security was over the top, but so were the people who used my facilities.

I approached a series of doors and heard shouts and cheers. It was as if the room I was about to enter was packed to the brim.

Ethan, the staff manager for the club, winced when he

caught sight of me coming in his direction. He leaned against the wall guarding access to the room.

He lifted his hands in the air. "I told everyone to go home after shift, but since Viper was in the cage, they all stayed to watch the match."

"How many people are there?"

"Umm. Less than a hundred."

"There better not be anywhere near that many people in there." I punched in the code and opened the lock before pulling the door open.

Immediately, the chaos and energy of a real match of athletes bombarded my senses.

As I moved into the arena, I could tell Ethan was dead wrong—there were at least a hundred people in here, if not more.

It was as if staff who weren't on the schedule to work had come in to watch the match.

I tapped a few shoulders to let them know I wanted to pass, and as soon as they saw me, they jumped out of the way.

Yep, all of them were going to hear from me at the meeting in the morning.

Slowly, I made my way through the crowd and reached the front.

My eyes focused on the men in the ring circling each other.

One in particular.

Kir.

He bobbed and weaved, blocking Dillon's punches and kicks. His body glistened with sweat, from his face to his bare toes.

Everything deep inside my core clenched, and my heartbeat accelerated.

I licked my lips.

Dear God. It was always like this—the visceral need for him.

I'd felt it that first night when I was barely twenty and walked into an underground fight club, and it was more so now.

Kir pivoted and landed a roundhouse kick to Dillon's shoulder. Dillon retaliated by punching Kir in the face and making me wince.

Damn, that looked as if it hurt.

They went back and forth all over the ring.

It was raw, edged with violence, and so fucking intense.

Kir had no idea how beautiful he was. The scars on his body only added to the raw danger and appeal of mixed martial arts.

God, I wanted to touch him, taste him, fuck him as I'd done countless times after a match. The adrenaline always made him wild and completely untamed. We'd go at it nearly all night.

My nipples beaded, my clit throbbed, and arousal pooled between my legs.

I was in so much trouble.

The bell rang, ending the round. And as if he'd sensed my presence and thoughts, Kir's eyes lifted to mine. I saw the same intense hunger I felt flash in his gaze.

This pull toward him was a desperate need I couldn't control. It overwhelmed me.

God, I ached for his touch.

Kir's attention shifted toward Dillon as he said something, effectively breaking the spell he had on me.

I released a deep breath.

I had to get out of here, or I'd do something that I was sure would get me in a hell of a lot of trouble.

Turning, I made my way out of the small arena and decided a date with my vibrator was the only way to resolve the situation I found myself in.

16

KIRAN

Around one o'clock in the morning, I entered the waterfront mansion I'd use as Antoni Silva in the Key Biscayne area of Miami. This place was everything I hated, ultra-modern, void of anything but tones of gray, black, and white, and cold. Why the hell someone wanted to live in something so sterile, I'd never understand.

Walking over to the bar, I poured myself a drink and then stepped out onto the patio overlooking the canal behind the house.

Lifting the glass for a sip, I couldn't help but wince as it touched my lips.

Nearly every muscle in my body ached, but I had no regrets. It had been months since I'd exerted that kind of energy in the ring and years since I'd had a no-holds-barred fight against someone who wouldn't pull any punches. Dillon wanted to make a point about not keeping family in the dark, and I need to let off some steam from my conversation with Jayna earlier in the day. Yeah, I'd had my ass handed to me, but it was well worth it.

Especially when I'd seen the way Jayna had all but eaten me up with her eyes. Why she loved to watch me fight was beyond my comprehension. MMA was violent and dirty, not something for a woman like her.

I'd known she was in the room from the beginning of the last round. It was as if my body sensed it. Then when she'd come up to the front, dressed in her tailored outfit, I felt as if I'd transported back eleven years.

She was polish and class, where I was the streets and unrefined. And she wanted me. I saw it then as I'd seen it tonight.

All my annoyance with her from earlier in the day had disappeared, replaced with the primal need to fuck her raw.

Shit. I had to stop thinking about sex.

I threw back the rest of the drink, letting the liquid burn down my throat and numb my senses.

Setting my tumbler down on a nearby table, I rolled up my shirtsleeves and leaned against the railing. What was she doing now? Would she be at one of her nightclubs or home?

On instinct, I pulled my phone from my pocket and dialed her number.

"Hi," she answered on the second ring.

"Are you home?"

"Just got in."

I looked out at the water and decided to do something I'd

imagined for the last three weeks. "Go to your bedroom and take off your clothes."

She was silent for a moment and I wasn't sure if she'd comply.

"Okay." Her voice was a bit husky. "I just need to know, who am I with right now?"

"Who do you want to be with, Princesa?"

"The man in the cage tonight. The one who used to fuck me until I could barely walk in the locker room after a match."

Fuck. She was going to kill me.

"Get naked, Jayna," I ordered as I moved to a lounger, sat back, and adjusted my hard cock in my pants.

"Yes, Kir." I heard the rustling of clothing. "Now what?"

"Lie down on your bed, switch the phone to video, and set it beside you at an angle where I can see you."

She came into view, her beautiful face flushed with arousal just from the idea of what we were about to do.

After gathering a few pillows, she had the phone positioned so I had a complete view of her long, curvy body.

"Stick your fingers in your mouth. Yes, like that. Now imagine it's my mouth and show me what I'd do to you."

She took her wet fingertips, rubbed them down her bottom lip, along the hollow of her neck, and between the valley of her breasts. She grasped a nipple, pinching it hard and then circling the areola.

"Kir," she cried out. "I ache."

"I know, baby. Show me where."

She squeezed her other breast and then slid her hands lower, gliding down her flat belly and then along the seam of her swollen pussy lips.

"Here. I ache here."

"Play with yourself. Show me what you do when you imagine it's my mouth as you get yourself off."

Her arousal glistened on her fingers as they glided between her folds and circled her clitoral nub. She circled and teased herself, writhing under the play of the rhythm she created.

I shifted, needing to grip my cock so I wouldn't come in my pants like some damn teenager.

"Oh God, Kir. This feels so good."

Her fingers rubbed back and forth, worrying the straining bundle of nerves. She squeezed her aching breast with her other hand, pinching the puckered nipple hard, so much harder than I expected.

"Spread your legs wider. I want to see your glistening cunt. Now push two fingers inside your pussy."

When she followed my direction and arched up, I nearly groaned.

She was a fucking living fantasy.

"Yes, like that." My voice was hoarse, filled with lust. "Pump in and out. That's it. Fuck yourself. Harder, Princesa. Push yourself to that edge."

"Oh God, Kir, I'm going to come. I need to come." Her gaze turned toward the camera.

"No, not yet. Let it build."

"Please let me come."

"No. Keep fucking yourself. You need to make yourself so wet that if I was between your legs, I could drink your need up with my mouth."

She bit her lips and threw back her head, arching up. She

bucked as she continued to fuck her fingers in and out of herself.

God, she was fucking beautiful. Face and body flushed with desire and need, nipples hard, pussy swollen and dripping.

There was no way I was going to last without coming in my pants. I unbuckled my belt and lowered my zipper.

"Kir. Oh fuck. I can't hold out. I just can't." She clenched her eyes closed and bucked against her pistoning fingers. "Oh God, oh God. Kir."

I freed my cock, fisting the base, and pumped. There was nothing like the perfection of my woman lost in pleasure.

"That's it, baby. Make it last," I gritted out, watching her ride out her release and feeling my own pushing forward.

Her eyes opened and focused on the screen next to her. Her breath caught as she realized what I was doing, and she licked her lips as a wicked glint entered her gaze. She pulled her fingers out of her pussy, licked them, and then shifted her body so the camera angle was directly between her legs and up her torso.

"You're trying to kill me." My voice was rough, and my ability to focus on anything other than the need to come was quickly slipping away.

I gripped my cock harder, sliding my palm up and down, and imagined it was the perfect wet cunt on the other side of the screen wrapped around me. Jayna's fingers pushed back inside her as her thumb rubbed the bundle of nerves at the apex of her sex.

"Fuck, Kir. I'm coming again," she cried out as she dug her heels into the bed, lifting her ass a fraction and giving me an even better view.

And that was all it took. My balls drew up and the first spasm rippled through my groin.

"Watch, Jayna."

Immediately she raised her head and licked her lips as cum erupted from the head of my dick. I gritted my teeth and continued to pump until every drop was out and then collapsed back onto the lounger.

When I could breathe again, I said, "Soon, I'm going to come inside you and not on my hand."

"That all depends on how proficient Antoni Silva is at seducing me."

"Baby, seducing you is going to be the easiest part of this whole plan."

"We'll see," she mumbled through a yawn.

I looked at the screen to find her now lying on her side. Her thick black hair tumbled around her pillow and sleep touched the edges of her eyes.

God, she was so beautiful.

A breeze picked up and I felt the cum drying on me. I reached to the side, grabbing a towel from a stack near the pool. Once I was clean, I tucked myself back into my pants and stood, grabbing my phone and making my way into the house and toward my bedroom.

"Kir?"

"Yes?"

"Do you like who I am now?"

"You're still the same."

"I'm stronger now. I can do things on my own."

"You were always strong. You've always done things on your own. I just came along for the ride."

She shook her head. "No. I depended on you too much. I used you as a shield."

"Why is that a bad thing? I wanted to protect you."

"Because I didn't know how to handle it when you weren't there. Now I can do things without depending on anyone." A tear slipped down her cheek, and my gut clenched.

I'd stayed away thinking I was protecting her, and hurt her more by failing to be there for her. Now she was keeping a barrier in our relationship, something I couldn't push past.

"I'm not going anywhere this time."

"I won't like it, but I can handle it if you do."

"Jayna, I mean it. I swear to you."

"We'll see." She grew quiet, just staring at the screen, her breath soft and steady.

After a few moments, she said, "I don't want you to be Antoni Silva."

"I don't want to be him either. He's a little too flashy for my taste."

"Mine too." Jayna smiled as her face grew a little sleepier. "Antoni's not my type."

"Is that right? Tell me who's your type."

She yawned again and then whispered, "I like the grumpy, brooding, hiding-in-the-shadows type who sneaks into my club and makes me come over video chat."

"Good to know."

"I think I should hang up now."

"Good night, my love."

She mumbled something and her lashes drifted shut.

I watched her relax into sleep for a few moments and then ended the call.

Setting my phone on the bathroom counter, I gripped my hair. I had to fix this mess with Jayna. I'd lost her trust and I had to prove that I'd never fail her again.

She wanted me, but not under some other name.

Nik thought it was as simple as walking back into my old life, but I knew it wasn't that easy.

But I'd pay whatever it cost to make it happen.

After a quick shower, I sent a text to my brothers.

KIR: After this plan plays out, get things ready. I'm coming back.

Almost immediately, Nik responded.

NIK: Already in the works. As I said, all you have to do is walk into the sunshine.

17

JAYNA

SIX WEEKS TO THE DAY SINCE I'D LEFT KIR ON THE ISLAND, I pulled up the driveway to my mother's beautiful waterfront mansion. Mummy had arrived late last night with Danika in tow to settle back into life in Miami. As far as everyone here knew, Mummy had canceled her trip with her friends to spend some time with Danika in New York and reconnect with the few people who'd stayed in touch with her after the horrible divorce from Papa.

Now that she was back, it officially meant that the pretending would soon be over.

Well, sort of.

Fuck.

Who was I kidding? The pretending was only beginning.

A pang of nervousness filled my belly.

Maybe it was the time apart but not apart that made me see things with Kir differently. He really wanted us to work. Every time he spoke of the future, he emphasized it.

He'd broken my trust in him when he let me believe he was dead.

I wouldn't deny that I was scared, but deep down, I wanted more and more for us to have a life together again.

But would it be as Kir and Jayna or as Antoni and Jayna?

It felt so strange knowing when I saw him next, we'd have to pretend that we were essentially strangers, that we hadn't touched each other, tasted each other, shared every part of each other, or recently watched each other come over video chat.

God, I couldn't believe we'd done that. Maybe it was the arousal of seeing him fight that had me so compliant when he'd ordered me to get naked. Then when I'd opened my eyes as I'd orgasmed and seen him working his cock with his fist, I'd wanted nothing more than to suck him off.

Shit. I had to put those thoughts away.

I brought my car to a stop and turned off the ignition, releasing a deep breath to calm my body. Once I had myself under control, I stepped out into the balmy ninety-degree summer heat. I nodded to my security detail, who pulled into the guesthouse area where I knew the housekeeper would have some food waiting for them.

Shielding my eyes from the sun with my hands, I took in the gorgeous house and landscape. Lush palm trees lined the sides of the property, and flowers and thick greenery decorated a path leading up to the front door.

God, I loved it here.

This was probably the only place in my childhood that ever

felt like home. The house had belonged to my maternal grandparents and was left to Mummy and her sisters after they'd passed away.

Here, there were no memories of beatings or screaming matches, no shadows of the girl who'd rebelled against the oppression of a father who was hell-bent on molding his only daughter into the perfect society debutante. In this place, there was a history of an indulgent grandfather and loving grandmother, summers filled with laughter, large family gatherings, friends who were welcome to visit, and a mother who smiled all the time.

It was crazy how two very affluent families could be so very different. How my grandfather must have regretted ever introducing his baby girl to Ashok Shah.

Shit, I was not going to let Papa into my head, not here.

I growled, grabbing my overnight bag from the backseat, and headed in the direction of the kitchen entrance of the house.

The second I opened the door, all of my irritation with myself disappeared. The sounds of Mummy chattering with Danika as she moved about cooking reached my ears and brought a smile to my lips.

"Come inside, Jayna," Mummy called from around the corner in Gujarati, my family's native language. *"I've made dinner. I want you to eat before you go out tonight."*

"Coming," I responded, setting down my bag and moving into the expanse of the giant open-concept kitchen.

I found Danika leaning over the island, standing on tiptoes as she spooned something into her mouth as Mummy stirred the pot.

They both were so beautiful.

Danika wore a cap-sleeve sky-blue dress that went to her knees and looked perfect on her petite, five-foot-one frame, and Mama was stylish as ever in her silver embroidered tunic-styled green top and black pants.

"It smells good in here. What did you make?"

"It's a fusion dish I created at Danika's house. Here, taste and tell me what you think."

As I approached, I couldn't help but internally shake my head at the enormity of the kitchen.

Everything in this space said a chef was in residence. Mummy loved to cook, and she loved her gadgets. Which meant she needed space for them. The original house design couldn't accommodate her needs, so she'd renovated it to her liking. Now, this place rivaled something found in a top restaurant with its two oversized islands, three sinks, and four ovens.

Who the hell needed four ovens?

My mother. But then again, the woman loved to feed people and entertained her friends here in Miami regularly.

I walked up to her and leaned in as she scooped up a bit of what looked like some kind of stew of vegetables from a pot, blew on it to cool it off, and then brought it to my lips. The taste was incredible. It had the traditional flavors of Indian cooking with garlic, coriander, and cardamom, but with the added hints of spices found in Southeast Asian dishes.

"Oh my God, that's good."

"See, I told you, Auntie. It's amazing."

"Both of you are biased."

Danika walked up to me, wrapping an arm around my waist and resting her head against my shoulder.

It was always like this with us. We were cousins, but she was more of a baby sister to me. From the moment Papa had brought her home as a frightened fourteen-year-old after her father's death, I'd had someone who understood our family and what it was like to not quite fit in.

Though I'd thought she'd had a head transplant for the longest time and become Papa's puppet. I'd learned later that she'd made herself indispensable to Papa to work out a plan to destroy him. A plan she'd given up to protect Nik. He was more important than her need for revenge.

It was amazing the things love made us do.

"I'm trying to convince her to write a cookbook." Danika looked up. "Maybe you'll have better luck."

"I doubt it. You tell me I'm stubborn. Where do you think I get it from?"

"Very funny. Sit, both of you. Eat. I know you're going to drink tonight. I don't want you passing out."

I almost laughed. That was Mummy. Never any judgment. She accepted me, my business, my life. She'd known what Kir was from the beginning and accepted him. Then again, she'd married a monster wrapped in civility and pedigree.

"You sure you don't want to come dancing with us and celebrate the opening of the club?"

"No. I'm too old for nightclubs."

"Believe me. You are not too old. Come on. We can make it a fun night."

She glared at me as if that was the stupidest idea she'd ever heard. "Tonight, you have other things to take care of as well.

Bring him here once this is all over. I will give my son-in-law a piece of my mind then."

Danika and I winced at the same time. Kir was going to get it from Mummy when she got a hold of him. Mummy had mourned him as much as everyone else had.

I wished I'd been the one to break the news to her about Kir, but the duty had gone to Danika. And, according to her, Mummy had accepted it pretty well, only muttering about idiot men on and off for a few days.

"You should call the *masis* over and have a ladies' night in," I suggested.

Masi in Gujarati meant auntie, more specifically, maternal aunt. Mummy had two sisters and five female first cousins. They all lived within the Miami area, so I referred to the collective as the *masis*. Mummy's whole extended family lived in Florida or somewhere in the southeastern United States.

"That is exactly what we are doing. They will be here later."

"Don't get too wild." Danika waggled her eyebrows. "You don't want the neighbors thinking Jayna brought her club to the house again."

When the women gathered, it was like seeing an insane group of fifty-somethings laughing, drinking, and telling the dirtiest of jokes. Half the time, I wasn't sure if I should be mortified or jump in.

Deep down, I was so happy that Mummy finally found some peace and joy after the life she'd lived in New York.

"Yes, let's not make the neighbors believe I threw a party in your upscale neighborhood. I already have a reputation," I said.

"I don't give a shit what anyone thinks. About you or me. They can go to hell, for all I care."

I stared at Mummy in open-mouthed shock. She'd just cussed. My sweet, never-say-a-mean-thing mom cursed.

I glanced at Danika, who seemed to be in the same stupor.

"Stop looking at me like that. Going back to New York made me realize I left that stupid judgmental life for good, and I will never let anyone make me feel worthless again. People who picked your father over me despite knowing he was abusing me and all because of his money and standing don't deserve a second thought.

"And anyone here who wants to make comments can go to hell too. Besides, my daughter is married to the heir of a Puerto Rican mafia family. If that isn't going to scare them into shutting up, then nothing else will."

"Ummm. Mummy." I walked up to her, taking her hands in mine. "Did something happen that you didn't tell me?"

She shook her head. "It doesn't matter. Just know I don't care what the media or anyone says about me. I don't want you to either."

That was when it hit me. Papa must have finally realized he wouldn't be able to force a renegotiation of the settlement since Mummy had no tangible assets in the States. Knowing him, he probably had someone say something to cut her while she was there.

Mummy and Papa's divorce had been one of the biggest scandals in the Indo-American affluent communities of the New York area. Papa had smeared Mummy's name, accusing her of everything from stealing to cheating but never owning the fact he abused her for nearly every day of their twenty-plus years of marriage. In the end, it had taken two years and the destruction of Mummy's reputation to get the divorce and another two years to get the final settlement.

"You have your party and make as much noise as you want. Just make sure the guards know what's going on."

She nodded.

"Also, please don't let anyone know Kir is alive or that bit about the mafia. It's all a cover story. Remember?"

"I know this." She rolled her eyes with a smirk, then her face sobered. "I need to ask you something."

"What?"

"Luke. What is he to you?"

I wanted to say nothing, especially after the crap he'd pulled at the club, but kept those thoughts to myself. Although he'd called several times to apologize and we'd come to an understanding about him staying out of my business, I couldn't help but still feel a bit salty about the whole incident.

I had no doubt that if I were a man, he'd never have pulled any of the shit he'd pulled with me.

Kir had his faults, but he'd always respected my intellect and business know-how. When I'd told Danika about the incident, she informed me that Luke was an asshole and would always remain an asshole. But then again, she'd disliked Luke since we were teens when he'd picked on her for being the poor relation. Something I told her was the behavior of an idiot teen and not the guy he was now. However, when Dani held a grudge, she held a grudge.

"He's a friend. Why?"

"Well, his father implied it's more."

And that had to be the person who upset Mummy while in New York City. Luke's father was an ass on a good day and he hated Mummy. He believed she was the reason I'd run away from home and refused the marriage contract. I wouldn't put it past him to have said something cutting to Mummy or started spreading some lie.

"It is completely platonic. I've made it very clear to Luke."

"Is he going with you tonight?"

"He's part of our friends' circle, so he's meeting up with our group. There are going to be at least a dozen of us there."

"Be careful. I don't trust that family."

I sighed. I understood Mummy's reservations. Even with Luke's recent behavior, he wasn't like his father.

"You have nothing to worry about with Luke. I can handle him."

"He wants more than friendship from you."

"He does and knows I'm not open to anything. He's accepted it."

I knew she wasn't convinced but she nodded.

"Okay. Eat. You need a full belly for all the alcohol. I'm going to call your *masis* and see when they're arriving." Mummy turned, leaving Danika and me alone.

"That was intense," Danika commented once she was sure Mummy was out of earshot.

"Yep. So, want to fill me in on what went down between yesterday and today?"

"I honestly have no idea. I spent most of my day working on a project and Auntie said she would run a few errands. When she came back, she was quiet but seemed fine. Well…" Danika thought for a moment. "No, she seemed determined, like she'd accepted something. Since I was trying to keep Nik from flying down with us and micromanaging our plans, I didn't focus on Auntie too much."

"I guess that's something the brothers have in common."

"They can try all they want—it's in their nature to make sure we're protected. As long as we don't let them walk all over us, there isn't a problem."

"Is that the key to it?"

"Yep. Kir thinks you're in danger because of him. For someone who lives his life protecting others, he feels as if he failed you."

"That's not true. If he'd never met me, he would never have had the accident. That was my fault."

"He doesn't see it that way."

"Kir and I have some issues to work through. That isn't one of them."

"Have you talked to him about…" She trailed off, knowing I'd catch on.

In all the conversations we'd had over the last few weeks, we'd touched every subject imaginable. Well, except for one.

I shook my head. "I'm not sure I can open that wound."

"Jay, you aren't the type of person to avoid things. Besides, the wound hasn't healed, no matter what you want to believe. That's the reason you haven't told him."

I remained quiet, knowing she was right. Danika had been there through most of it, even when the worst of it had overwhelmed me.

"What if I tell him and it makes it worse?"

Dani moved to where I stood and wrapped an arm around my waist. "You already know the answer to that question."

We'd go our separate ways when this charade ended.

"I still love him, Dani." I leaned my chin against the top of her head

"You wouldn't have done any of this if you didn't."

"Sometimes, I hate being an adult."

"Our childhood wasn't a walk in the park. If given a choice, I'll take being an adult. I get to break into people's private information, and you get people drunk and let them beat each other up for our livings."

I laughed, feeling the heaviness of the previous conversation lift.

"True, but not exactly in that order." I moved to the stove and filled a bowl with the fusion stew Mummy had made. "Let's eat. Then I'll show you the jewel of Miami nightlife."

18

Kiran

"This is some place she has here," Joel said as we sat in the VIP section of Hira, Jayna's nightclub in the more industrial section of Miami Beach. "But then again, she's created a niche for herself with these clubs."

"She knows the market and delivers the fantasy that people want," I responded and then shook my head as he smiled at the tall brunette server who set our drinks down in front of us.

"That she does."

"You're working, remember?"

"Doesn't mean I can't appreciate a beautiful woman when I see one. Besides, the second your pretty lady comes into view, you're going to forget anyone exists."

"I'm not going to deny it."

I hadn't touched her in six weeks and I felt as if I were a man dying of thirst.

How the hell had I gone years without her?

Joel glanced at his watch. "She'll arrive in a few minutes. I suggest you get into position. Just make sure our guys have an eye on you at all times and keep your face in the shadows."

There was a warning in his statement as if he would punch me if I disappeared with Jayna.

"I hear you."

I threw back my drink and I stood, adjusting my shirt.

Working my way around the lounge and toward the central area of the club, I took a set of stairs leading up to the second level. I approached a bar nestled into a corner, ordered a drink, and continued around the room until I reached my designated position.

It was amazing how this damn plan had made it easier and easier to accept my scars were just part of who I was now. I'd noticed the way the bartender had looked at me, but it hadn't bothered me as it would have only a few weeks ago.

Well, at least there was some benefit to being the flashy Antoni Silva. The people who interacted with him had to view him as ruthless and completely comfortable with who he was, something I'd been exactly like back in the day. It seemed as if it was coming back.

I sipped my drink and leaned against the railing.

From this vantage point, I could see directly down into the heart of the club and the hallway leading from the employee entrance.

The lights shifted from a deep red to white and gold, and at the same time, the celebrity DJ came into view on the stage.

The crowd cheered and shouted, losing themselves in the Latin hip-hop sounds filling the room.

Damn, this place was really incredible. There was no doubt Jayna knew this business inside and out.

Jayna had always had a knack for spotting the perfect and most profitable locations for every one of her clubs. Usually, someplace experts would have told her would never work. And every single time, she'd proven them wrong and turned a profit within a year or two.

When it came to business, I knew better than to mess with Jayna. Very few people wanted to see the intelligence behind the breathtaking face and vixen body. People assumed Danika was the smart one in the family, with her hacker mind, but when it came to numbers, calculations, and stats, Jayna took the prize.

She could run the calculations for profit or loss within seconds based on minimal information. She also could remember stats on fighters and tell me the likelihood of them winning a match or not. She'd come in handy a time or two when betting on matches in Vegas.

It amazed me how she'd turned my underground fight club into a business with high-dollar purses, sponsors, and fighters who were actual athletes.

Hell, she'd taken that whole concept and turned it into the Ladai Room clubs.

I pulled out my phone as it buzzed with an incoming text.

JOEL: Their car just arrived. You're on. Don't fuck it up.
KIR: Thanks for the words of encouragement.
JOEL: Anytime.

The last thing I wanted to do was fuck it up more than I already had.

Over the last few weeks, Jayna and I'd grown closer, but there was a wall I couldn't punch through, no matter how hard I tried. I couldn't fix the mistakes of the past if she refused to talk about them.

It was frustrating, but then I understood her apprehension. She was scared.

Hopefully, the steps I took would be enough for her to see that I wouldn't fail her again.

Tossing back the rest of my drink, I let the amber liquid slide down my throat and readied myself to find my princess.

Jayna

A LITTLE BEFORE ELEVEN O'CLOCK, DANIKA AND I ARRIVED AT the back entrance of Hira. Nestled along a corner of Miami Beach considered "lower class" by the other venues, it had given me the perfect location to develop my unique club.

"Now I get what you meant by the jewel of your nightclubs," Danika said as she took in the name written with laser lighting on the brick building.

Hira, translated from Gujarati, meant diamond. I named all of my clubs after precious jewels. It started as a joke between Kir and me because of his nickname for me. And since princesses had lots of gems, my club names were born.

Dillon approached the car, opening the door. "Hello, ladies. Most of our party is already inside."

As we stepped out of the car, I scanned the area. Security directed traffic all around the area, moving it away from the overflowing parking lots, and the line to enter the club wrapped around the side of the building.

"Wow. I wasn't expecting this level of insanity."

"Get real," Danika said. "Everyone knows the opening of your clubs is like a Vegas production."

"Whatever." I looked at Dillon. "Is everyone in place inside?"

Dillon leaned toward my ear and whispered, "Nothing to worry about."

I exhaled, tucked my arm into Danika's, and moved in the direction of the security guard who waited for us.

I couldn't help the pang of anxiety churning through my stomach, especially knowing tonight Kir and I would be seen in public together for the first time in years.

No, not Kir. Antoni Silva.

Pushing down all the nervousness, I stepped into the dimly lit hallway leading toward the employee lounge.

Danika trailed her fingers along the textured wallpaper. "I love the feel of this."

I smiled. Everything in my clubs appealed to the five senses: sight, sound, smell, taste, and touch.

From the drinks made of exclusive spirits to the scent in the air to the music, the lighting, and the walls, I wanted anyone who stepped into my place to lose themselves in the experience.

My nightclubs were the first things I ever created without input from anyone. I'd seen a need in the market for them and decided to use my inheritance from my maternal grandparents to fill it. It hadn't been easy to get the first one off the ground, but I'd done it.

Everyone in my Indo-American community thought I'd lost my mind and was rebelling against Papa. No proper daughter of Ashok Shah would have opened up a series of nightclubs catering to decadence and sin.

When in fact, it had nothing to do with him. He hadn't even been a thought in my mind during any of the planning. I'd created a business that I loved. Hell, I'd started multiple businesses that had nothing to do with the bastard who'd given me part of my genetics.

Of all my clubs, this one in particular was my favorite. Working on the build-out for this place had given me the push I needed to move forward with my life. Flying back and forth from NYC allowed me to focus on something other than everything I'd lost. Plus, it had allowed me to develop my plan and then the build-out for the Ladai Room venture I had today.

As we made our way into the club's main area, Danika paused, taking in the sights and sounds around her.

"Holy fuck."

I couldn't help but grin.

"Are the chandeliers moving?"

"Yep."

Everything in the club had a purpose, from the multitude of chandeliers to the exposed beams and the scaffolding. The proper lighting and shifting of various aspects of the room would change the ambiance to a completely different vibe.

This club had four different party rooms. I'd just come from one of them, the VIP lounge where those with deep pockets and a need for privacy could be part of the club but with a more relaxed atmosphere. Then there was the main room—it was a massive two-level space featuring eight bars, a giant dance floor on the bottom, and floating DJ and performer stages. It was visual enchantment at its best. The two remaining rooms consisted of a rave-style room with its own music, lights, and production style, and an open-air terrace that looked out over South Beach.

"Tell me why the hell I didn't invest in this place when you offered me the opportunity?"

"Because up until eight months ago, you were playing Papa's lapdog."

She winced. "Oh yeah. I try to block out that part of my memories."

"Yeah, it was pretty traumatic for a lot of us. I thought an alien had possessed your body for a short time."

"Asshole."

Dillon heard our exchange and chuckled. "Ladies, I'm going to make a quick call and meet you at our table."

As Dillon disappeared into the crowd, I turned to Danika. "Do you want to drink or dance?"

"Dance. We haven't enjoyed a night out in forever."

I offered her my hand. "Follow me."

She slid her palm over mine and I led her around the main room to the central dance floor. One of my floor bouncers inclined his head as he saw me approach and cleared a path in the crowd for Danika and me.

"Must be nice to be the boss," Danika said as we danced our way to the perfect spot under one of the lifted stages.

I grinned. "It has its perks."

The music shifted to a popular song played on the local

stations, and the floor filled with more and more people. I loved this. When the beat pulled the crowd in, and all anyone wanted to do was lose themselves in the rhythm.

Danika and I danced and laughed like we hadn't done in what seemed like forever. By the time the song finished, sweat tinged my skin, and I was nowhere near ready to leave the floor.

The lights shifted and I nudged Danika to look up at the performers. Acrobats jumped from various platforms as dancers moved from stage to stage.

"That's insane. Cool as hell, but insane."

"I know."

"Like I said, totally Vegas."

As the performance ended, everyone started dancing again, and I found myself facing a tall, well-dressed, and built man in front of me.

"I'm James. Care to dance?" He offered his hand.

James was exactly the type of guy I would have gone for back in the day, polished and refined. That was before I'd gone to an underground fight on a dare and stepped into a world where men lived on the edge and had no qualms with using their fists to make a living.

Just as I was about decline James's offer, I felt a tingle go down my spine and I knew without a doubt that Kir was behind me.

James glanced over my head and something passed in his blue eyes that looked almost like fear but then disappeared. "My bad. I didn't realize she was taken."

James seemed to all but run from the dance floor.

Kir couldn't have scared him that bad. Then I thought about

it. Kir wasn't a small man, and with the scars, he had a bit of an edge that might frighten some people.

"Mrs. King. I believe we're overdue for a dance."

When I remained still, Kir's large hand slid over my abdomen, both possessive and comforting, reminding me too much of the way it felt when he made love to me.

Goosebumps prickled my skin as he stepped closer, grazing his fingertips up one arm, over my shoulder, and along my neck.

I held in a moan.

Only this man had this kind of effect on me.

"I think I'll go back to the table. Enjoy your dance." Danika winked and disappeared into the crowd.

"Jayna." The deep rasp of my name on his tongue sent a spasm deep in my core. "Turn around."

Slowly, I shifted to face him. Dear God, he was gorgeous.

He wore a black shirt rolled up at the sleeves and dark denim jeans. The tattoos on his neck and arm were on full display, giving him the lethal edge I so loved.

"You clean up well."

"Anything for you, Mrs. King."

Taking my hand, he led me deeper into the crowd. The music barely registered. All I could focus on was this man whose presence took over my sense better than anything I could achieve with my clubs.

When we engulfed ourselves in the middle of the moving bodies where no one could decipher us from anyone else, he pulled me close, the front of my body flush against his.

The intensity of his gaze was so hot that I felt it all the way to my core.

"It's been a while, but I think I've still got it." He started moving his hips in that wicked way that always surprised me and gave me the dirtiest of thoughts.

He knew how to move, how to lead, how to make a woman feel consumed by his presence. He'd get me so hot, I'd all but drag him to some hidden corner of my club to make me come.

I wanted so desperately to run my fingertips across the stubble on his jaw and draw him close for a kiss. Instead, I placed my palms on his sculpted shoulders and followed his lead to the rhythm of the music. Kir's palms settled on my hips and worked their way around my curves, bringing back all the memories of how we'd danced over the years at my other clubs.

We knew each other's bodies, the way we moved. We were in sync.

My fingers slid into his hair and I arched backward. He pressed his hand against the bare skin revealed by the low neckline of my dress and then glided up until he was cupping my throat.

His possessive hold sent a flood of arousal between my legs.

My breath grew shallow, and there was no hiding the arousal I felt.

He guided me back up, keeping the pressure on my neck. We stared into each other's eyes, lust and need pushing us.

Before I could do something stupid and beg him to fuck me in one of the backrooms, the rhythm of the music changed, and immediately we adjusted to the tempo without missing a beat.

Every nerve in my body felt as if it had fired to life. I'd danced with other men at my other clubs, but it was never like this—all-consuming, where I only saw this mesmerizing man.

"It's just as intense as it always was," Kir said as he shifted me so my back was to his front.

"Yes, it is." I reached up, gripping the back of his neck and rocking my ass against his jeans-covered cock. "It's because dancing is like sex. And sex with us has always been intense."

"We probably shouldn't have danced. Anyone who sees us will know we are more than strangers, if not lovers."

His words brought reality crashing back, and I stiffened. "Oh fuck."

Kir turned me to face him, sliding a hand around my waist and continuing to dance as the music drifted to a slower beat. "Don't worry. This plays into the cover."

"How?" I gripped his shoulders and frowned up at him.

"Well, you're supposed to start an affair with Antoni Silva." He leaned down until his lips were a breath away from mine. "We can just accelerate the schedule."

I wanted to close the distance and taste him but resisted the urge. If I followed through, it would mean more than I could handle right now, and we still hadn't worked through some of my deepest pain.

"So, skip the dating altogether?" I looked up into his dark eyes.

"We've had a date nearly every night for the last month."

"That was Kir and Jayna, not Antoni and Jayna."

"We're one and the same. For our purposes, just think of it like you're having an affair with my alter-ego."

"And when did this affair start?"

"Six weeks ago, on an island in the Keys."

"Doesn't an affair mean we're having sex?"

His lips turned up at the corners. "What would you call what happened over video chat the other night?"

God, he was so handsome. "Foreplay."

"In that case, why not keep up the sexual tension." He leaned forward, rubbing his stubble against my cheek and then along my jaw as his hand slid up to the lower swell of my breast.

Goosebumps immediately prickled my skin and I held in a moan.

Fuck, I was in so much trouble.

"You're really good at this."

"Good at what?" he asked, knowing what he was doing to my body.

"Seduction."

"Only with you. I know you, baby. Maybe soon you'll believe that I've always seen you." He pulled back and released me, breaking the spell he'd had on me. "Have dinner with me."

"When?"

"Every night for the rest of my life." He grinned, knowing how cheesy he sounded.

"You're ridiculous." I laughed and shook my head. "Let's start with Sunday night and then I'll see about the rest."

This would give me enough time to handle Hira's opening and build the courage to have the discussion I needed to have with him.

"It's a date. A real one." He took my hand and lifted it, kissing my knuckles before turning and disappearing into the crowd of dancers.

I stood there for a few moments, trying to calm my emotions and body down. There was no way I could go to my table without giving away how I was feeling.

At that moment, I glanced in the direction of the VIP lounge and spotted a few of my girlfriends. They waved and started hooting and hollering. Then I saw Luke standing off to the side. He leaned against the railing, drinking something out of a glass.

My heartbeat shot up.

Had he seen Kir's face?

I released a relieved breath as I realized it was too dark to make out faces unless you knew who to look for. Plus, Kir had his back to the lounge the whole time we danced.

Knowing it was time to go, I weaved my way through the crowd and up the stairs leading to the landing where my group was waiting for me.

As I approached, Luke stalked past me, saying, "That was some dance. Good thing you're not open to dating anyone," and then went down the stairs.

Well, shit.

I'd told Luke I wasn't interested in anyone, and there I was, so lost in my dance that anyone who saw me would know I wasn't dancing with a stranger but a lover.

Danika came toward me with a cocktail. "Don't worry about him. He's been in a piss-poor mood ever since the girls told him you were dancing with a hottie."

"That's just great." I took the drink, sipped, and closed my eyes, enjoying the perfect blend of flavors.

I honestly had the best bartenders. They never missed a beat.

"He had a chance to dance with his own hotties. He could have gone down with the guys when they went trolling, but he stayed here." Danika set a hand on my arm. "Something's up with him."

"What do you mean?"

"He was asking the girls way too many questions about you for a friend who hangs out with you all the time."

"I think you're reading too much into it."

"Whatever. I think he's too nosey."

"That's because you have a bias."

"I won't deny it." Danika downed her drink and signaled for a round of shots. "Okay, enough serious talk. I want to have fun. Time to get drunk."

She started dancing with my other girlfriends around us.

"Nik is going to kill me for contributing to your delinquency."

"What he doesn't know won't hurt him."

I loved this woman.

I laughed and decided to join my cousin in letting loose for the rest of the night.

Picking up a shot from a tray a server placed on our table, I lifted it in the air. "Bottoms up."

19

KIRAN

An hour after leaving Jayna at the club, I drove my car to the gates of what I now called "the Silva compound." The place wasn't ugly by any means, but nothing like the beautiful home I'd built for Jayna on our island. The ultra-modern, white concrete house with giant walls surrounding the acre-and-a-half property fit perfectly into the affluent neighborhood of multimillion-dollar homes but completely clashed with my style.

How the fuck Sam found this place on such short notice, I'd never figure out. But then again, he had a head for real estate that boggled the mind.

As I pushed the button on my car's console to access the gate, a wave of uneasiness prickled my senses.

Something wasn't right. As if the moment I walked into the house, someone would ambush me.

I glanced around the property as I went up the driveway, and the restlessness in my senses grew.

I reached under my seat, opened the hidden compartment, and pulled out the pistol tucked away for situations like this. Years working as the King enforcer had trained me to stay prepared for shit to go down at any moment.

Arin had taught me to always go with my gut.

The one damn time I hadn't, I'd gotten into the wreck that had changed the course of my life.

Not happening again.

I pulled into the garage, turned off the ignition, and then sent an alert to Joel and my security team. We'd planned for scenarios like this, and they'd know what to do.

I tucked the gun into the back waistband of my jeans and opened the car door, making my way inside the house.

It was too quiet.

There should be some noise from the patrol crew that worked on the ground level near the docks. Hopefully, they were only knocked out, and nothing worse had come of them.

There was only one person who'd go to all this trouble to get to me.

Hector.

I'd expected a meeting. Hell, I'd set everything in motion to force some form of confrontation.

But not tonight.

I was going to kick my brothers' asses for not telling me the dipshit had left Puerto Rico.

This was going to be a long fucking night.

Making my way into the dark, open living room, I spotted what I could only assume was Hector's shadowy figure sitting on one of my recliners. Immediately I pulled my gun, pointing it in his direction. At the same time, six other men pointed their guns at me.

Hector switched on a light and came into view. The resemblance we shared was striking. If it wasn't for our differing skin tones and eye colors, we'd look like brothers. There was no doubt we were related.

"*Hello, cousin,*" Hector said in Spanish before switching to accented English. "I see you've come back from the dead."

I held my gun toward him, not caring that I had six others angled at me. "I never died."

"I know. I'm not stupid. No body, no death. Victor Silva 101. But you wouldn't know that since you never knew *Abuelo*. Whereas I was raised at his knee and learned everything he knew."

"And yet, he still chose me as his heir." I slowly moved toward him, keeping my pistol trained at his head.

Hector gave no outward reaction to my dig except the slight clenching of his jaw. "Are you claiming it then? You planning to take over the Silva Familia?"

"It all depends."

Hector's men crowded toward me, but a lift of his finger had them pausing.

"On what?" Hector asked, his eyes narrowing.

I inclined my chin toward him. "You. Stay away from my wife and family, which means keep out of the States."

"Are those your requirements?"

"Yes."

"Are you saying you aren't establishing a territory here?"

"I'll make the decision after I get your answer."

"I find that hard to believe. Why create Antoni Silva? Why buy the port where my product is delivered?"

"To get your attention."

"Well, you have it."

"Then are we in agreement?"

"Not even close. First, I don't have any more need of your wife. That first contract did its job."

I narrowed my gaze. "You didn't get her."

"It did its job nonetheless. You're here." He leaned forward. "And second, do you actually believe I'm going to let you take over the mainland?"

"There is no *let* in the equation. I've already done it. My brothers and I call in a few favors and your whole operation goes down. No more Hector Estefan. The only name anyone will hear is Antoni Silva. Your whole operations worldwide will end."

"Are you threatening me?" Hector shifted as if to come toward me but then remained on the sofa.

"Let's call it a fact."

"You seem very confident for a man who hides in the shadows."

"When one is in the shadows, they have time to observe."

"Then why didn't you see me coming for your wife?"

I clenched my jaw. "Because the rules in our world state we keep wives and children out of it. I assumed you would keep to the protocol."

"What kind of bullshit world are you living in? This isn't some gentlemen's club." Hector shook his head. "When someone threatens my standing, those 'rules,' as you call them, go out the window."

"You have no standing on the mainland. Antoni Silva is the one in charge."

"I'm the one with the advantage here, cousin. I could shoot you right here, right now, and my problems are all solved. No more Antoni Silva, no more Kiran King."

"Is that what you believe?" I held his gaze. "Look down at your shirt."

At that moment, a series of red dots appeared on his shirt, and I knew the same was true for Hector's men.

Thank God Joel had taken no chances. It was dumb luck that I remembered *Tia* Martha saying Hector liked to talk. It had given Joel enough time to bring in the backup team.

"Well, fuck." Hector threw his head back and laughed as if he hadn't a care in the world. "You do have some of *Abuelo* in you, after all."

This guy was seriously demented.

"The tables have turned. Tell your men to stand down, and I'll tell mine."

Hector nodded and the six men lowered their weapons.

Within the next few seconds, Joel and my security team came through the balcony doors. They kept their guns pointed in Hector's direction.

"I thought you said you were going to tell your men to stand down," Hector said, glaring at me.

I lowered my gun, and Joel and the team followed but stayed near Hector's men.

Tucking my pistol back into my waistband, I took the seat across from Hector. "Before we begin our negotiations, I'm going to tell you a story. When I finish, listen to my offer. The power I have as Kiran King is ten times that of Antoni Silva."

"*Abuelo* hated Arin King. He believed Arin was the reason you turned your back on the family."

"No, Arin is the reason I have a family. I don't want your life, Hector. It suits you, not me. You are the true Silva heir."

Something passed in his eyes that I couldn't completely understand. Maybe it was acceptance that I was a King, not a Silva.

Who knew?

"Tell me your story, cousin. And then we discuss who carries the Silva Familia."

Over the next twenty minutes, I relayed my history, not the one the public knew through the media channels Arin had allowed when he'd adopted us, but the truth. Of how I'd run from foster care after my last foster father had beaten me for spilling soda in the kitchen. Of how Nik found me in an alley and helped me join his gang. Of how we ran our scams in the neighborhood. Of the night we tried to rob Arin King, and instead of killing us, he took us in and made us his sons. Then I went into details about Jayna, telling Hector about her background and what she meant to me.

"So let me get this straight. More than getting back to your life as Kiran King of the King brothers, you want to get back to your life with your wife. This is all about your wife." Hector shook his head. "For a fucking woman?"

"The right woman."

"Look, I get wanting revenge on those who took your life from you. It even makes sense to go after them for killing your child, but all this shit for a woman?"

Ignoring his outrage, I said, "Now to the deal. I don't want anything to do with the family. It's yours on a few conditions."

"Yes, I know, you want the mainland."

"Plus your assurance that neither you nor your allies will target any of the Kings or the stateside family."

"You want us to protect you?"

"Let's call it an exchange of favors. For my terms, you have complete control of the Silva Familia. No claiming Victor Silva's legacy again. You can even take on the Antoni Silva name, for all I care. You will also gain access to some of the King partners in South America and Asia. We know you are planning to expand in that direction."

A flicker of surprise flashed in his green eyes. "So, it's true then."

"What's true?"

"*Abuelo* always said Arin King played tough but stepped back when it came to getting his hands dirty. I guess the King brothers are the same."

"We don't pretend to be anything other than what we are. We are ruthless businessmen. Why exert unnecessary energy when calling in a favor garners us an army? In the end, the results are the same."

A calculating smile touched Hector's lips. "How will I know you aren't going to turn around and pull this Antoni Silva shit again?"

"You don't. That's where our agreement comes into play. Kings never go back on their word. That is the reason the price is high when others do."

"Yes, I've heard how you do things. My way is cleaner. Shoot the fuckers and be done with it. You Kings draw it out and let them suffer for all to see."

"At least they're alive."

Hector looked over his shoulder and gestured to the bar along the inner wall of the house. Immediately, one of his men went over and filled two glasses with some scotch and brought them over.

Hector picked up his tumbler and took a deep gulp, savoring the liquor, and then said, "Before I can agree to anything, I have a term to add."

"I'm listening."

"I want you to make it so no one can dispute my claim to the family. You saying I have it won't do."

"How do you propose I do this?"

"Figure out a way to make me legitimate. My parents were engaged when my mother died. Make it so they were married. *Abuelo*'s will says the eldest legitimate male heir. It doesn't say you by name. I'm the eldest."

"What makes you believe I have the means even to make this a possibility?"

"Just as I have sources, you have yours. Make my terms a reality and we have a deal."

20

JAYNA

"Do you want to come up?" I asked as Kir's car pulled up to the front of my Miami Beach high-rise a little before midnight.

He'd taken me on the date we'd discussed at the club. However, instead of a simple dinner as I'd expected, he'd reserved every table in one of the most exclusive restaurants in Miami and had the head chef give us private cooking lessons.

Cooking was something we both enjoyed and something I'd barely indulged in since Kir's accident. Extended time in the kitchen always triggered painful memories, but tonight, it was as if the weight on my shoulders was lifted.

It was the first time in close to three years that I'd genuinely laughed and enjoyed myself. Kir had picked the right thing to do to make our date perfect.

Kir shifted the car into park and faced me. "Are you sure you want to be alone with me? Aren't you the one who said we couldn't keep our hands off each other when we're alone?"

"I did say that." I smiled. "Do you have a problem with it?"

His eyes heated, and a shiver went down my spine. "None whatsoever. Just know by taking this step, your reputation as the Widow King is thoroughly ruined."

"Wasn't that the plan from the beginning, Mr. Silva?"

Kir set a hand on my thigh. "Jayna, if you want to figure out a different way, we can."

"Until you walk out in public as Kiran King, this is the only choice." I stared into his eyes. "Besides, Jayna Shah never cared about her reputation when she picked a King brother as her lover. Why should she start now?"

Kir cupped my face and leaned forward. I held my breath, thinking he was going to kiss me. God, I wanted it so much. Instead, he brushed his lips against my forehead.

"You humble me. I don't deserve you, but I'm never giving you up."

"Kir," I whispered.

The possessive way he'd said those words made my heart ache. I knew if I decided this wasn't something I could do, he'd let me go.

It was better to keep that box of pain locked away than risk the progress we'd made. My fear was that Kir would push me too far, and I'd snap.

He pulled back.

Something I couldn't understand passed in his gaze but disappeared just as fast. "Show me the way into this vertical garden structure."

As I guided Kir into the garage, I looked at the architecture and realized his description was very accurate. The high-rise my penthouse resided in looked like a glass-and-wood building growing out of a tropical rainforest. I'd picked the place because of its spectacular views of the ocean and city skylines and for the fact it was so different from everything I had in New York City.

The second we pulled into the area of my private elevator, three of my security team stepped out. The looks they were giving Kir's car as he parked next to mine almost had me laughing.

"Are you ready to say hello to some familiar faces?" I asked Kir.

"How would any of your Miami team know who I am?"

"This is our team from home. They came down with Danika to relieve my local crew for a few weeks."

"Fuck," Kir muttered, clenching his fists on the steering wheel. "There is something you need to know about them."

"I already know. I saw the video remember? I knew who was there during your accident."

It hurt to know that so many people knew Kir was alive when I was grieving. The team had helped Nik move Kir's body and stage the accident scene to make it look as if he'd died.

This was also probably why the team was so hyper-protective of me after the stabbing. They hadn't been there during my attack because they were with Kir, protecting him during his recovery. I'd had an alternative team during that time, one who was getting used to my routine.

When they had come down with Danika, I'd made my feeling on the past clear. Each of them accepted my views and then informed me they would take over my security indefinitely. They felt as if they'd failed me again because of the incident from a few weeks ago.

Damn, I was surrounded by overprotective people.

"Are you mad at them?"

"I'm not. They were doing their jobs."

"What about me?"

"A small part of me is salty that you didn't think I'd have put the pieces together by now." I glanced at him. "It seems as if there are many factors in this whole fucked-up situation that I won't discover until I stumble on them."

"So, in other words, yes."

I stared at him. I guessed I was going to have to get used to knowing that I'd lived in the dark while people close to me knew the truth about Kir.

It hurt.

Then again, the logical part of me wanted to say there were too many factors out of everyone's control.

Sometimes all I wanted to say was, fuck logic.

I needed a drink.

"Let's go up. We can discuss this in my place." I opened my door and stepped out into the garage.

Kiran came out on his side, staring after me. I moved toward the elevator leading up to my penthouse.

"Mrs. King, will you need an escort up?" Fox, the head of all of my security, said.

I studied him and saw the wariness in his eyes as Kir stepped up behind me. I almost wanted to laugh that the giant, nearly six-and-a-half-foot tall man was scared of me.

"Stop worrying. We had our talk. I'm not going to ream you again."

Fox relaxed and then looked over my shoulder. "I assume Mr. Silva is taking you up."

"Yes, we need to clear a few things up."

"Understood." Fox pushed the elevator button and the doors opened.

Kir and I stepped inside, neither of us saying anything. He leaned against one side of the cab, watching me. I knew he expected me to blow up. Instead, I took a similar stance against the railing at my back and held his gaze.

"You look as if you want to punch me."

"The thought did cross my mind, but you'd probably think it was foreplay."

"You're the one who likes it rough." His lips curved slightly at the corner, sending a flutter to my core and making me forget my irritation with him for a moment.

Just a moment.

"The way I'm feeling right now, I want to draw blood. Are you up for that kind of play?"

He moved toward me, grasping my throat and squeezing in that way that made my mind cloud with lust. "It wouldn't be the first time I've borne your marks."

My pulse hammered, and I set my hands against his chest, ready to push him away, but my fingers curled into his shirt, drawing him closer.

I held in a moan as the thick press of his cock rubbed against the juncture of my aching sex.

"Is that what you want? To bear my marks."

He rubbed his stubble-covered jaw along the side of my neck. "You put your mark on my soul a decade ago."

I closed my eyes, loving the feel of him on my skin.

"I have a question for you." Kir lifted his head and stared into my eyes. "What do you want to do first, fight or fuck?"

I licked my lips and watched his pupils dilate, the black swallowing the brown of his irises.

The smart thing to do would be to clear up everything that still hung between us, all the things we still hadn't let free. Then again, smart seemed to be a concept that disappeared when this man was so near me, touching me, seducing me as only he'd ever done.

The palm on my throat slid down the column of my neck and between the valley of my breasts as Kir's other hand gripped my hip, working the hem of my minidress higher.

"Do you have an answer for me, Princesa?"

At that moment, the elevator opened into the foyer of my penthouse.

I reached up, threading my fingers into his thick hair. "I want to fuck."

"Thank God." Kir lifted me against him by my thighs, and I immediately wrapped my legs around his waist.

He carried me barely into the front hallway when he pinned me to the wall and trailed his mouth along my jaw and neck.

"I have to fuck you now. We'll go slow later."

"I have no problems with that." I bit his ear as I pulled his shirt from his slacks and grazed my nails over the hot skin of his abdomen.

He hissed and clasped my wrists above my head while holding me against the wall with his thighs.

"Claws later. Right now, I need my cock buried deep in your cunt."

"I hope you aren't going to forget foreplay."

He released my hand, slid his fingers between my legs to my soaked underwear, and stroked up and down the seam.

He lifted a brow. "We've had six weeks of foreplay. I believe you are good and ready."

Grabbing the crotch of my thong, Kir tore the lacy material from my body and threw it onto the floor.

My core clenched and flooded, needing him to fill me. I'd spent years without him and now that he was here, six weeks felt like a lifetime.

I couldn't live without this man who'd broken my heart and ruined me for anyone else. I needed him so much—his touch, his kisses.

God, I needed his kisses.

"Kir," I whimpered and cupped his face, lifting my lips to his. "Please, I need you to kiss me."

He held himself still. "I want to. You have no idea how much I want to. But until there is no holding back of any kind between us, I won't kiss you."

I closed my eyes and let my legs slide to the floor, knowing the spell of lust was broken. I let my breath calm and then looked up at Kir.

"I'm not the only one holding back," I said, pushing past him and walking into the open space of my living room.

"Just because I didn't tell you Fox knew about me doesn't mean I was holding back. It honestly never crossed my mind until today. All I've ever wanted was to be with you, to protect you."

I whirled around. "That's bullshit. Every time I turn around, I discover someone else knew about your existence. Do you know how much that pisses me off?"

He gripped the back of his neck. "Only those who were there that night and my Solon contacts knew about me—none of Nik, Sam, or Rey's people, none of Danika's. I'm good at what I do. If I don't want someone to see me, they won't."

"And I was one of them."

"You already know why I did what I did. I was in a dark place. I was dangerous to be around. I'd rather you believed I was dead than see the monster I'd become."

I shook my head. "I don't accept that excuse. Do you have any idea what it was like?"

"I don't because you won't tell me. I've asked you over and over to tell me, but you won't."

"Was it something you wanted to hear over the phone?"

"Well, I'm here now. Tell me."

I could feel my body shake. I knew it was time. But I hated going to that place. The darkest part of my life. When I was so lost. Where a different Jayna existed.

"I need some air." I walked toward the glass doors of the wraparound balcony, opened them, and stepped outside.

I had to collect my thoughts.

I lifted my face into the warm, humid air and looked out at the night sky over the ocean.

I'd come so far. I was so much stronger now.

I could do things on my own. My life wouldn't depend on another person ever again.

"Are we ever going to talk about it?" Kir asked as he

approached me, and he set his hands on my hips. "Please, let me in."

My shoulders stiffened, and I resisted the urge to push away from him. I felt cornered, knowing this would always be the one thing that held me back from him.

What would happen to me if I told him and he disappeared again?

You'll survive as you've already done.

Panic filled my gut. "I thought I could do this. I'm not sure I can."

I shifted from his hold and paced as I pressed my fingertips to my eyes.

"Talk to me." He moved toward me, but I lifted my hands, staying him.

"I don't want to think about it. I had to work so hard not to think about it. I still work at it."

"I need to know."

Anger filled me. "Why? Why is it so important for you to know? It was my pain, not yours."

"She was my little girl too."

I stalked over to him, shoving him back.

"What do you want me to say? That I was scared out of my mind, thinking I would have to raise a baby without you?"

Shove.

"Or that I knew she'd died the second the mugger stabbed me?"

Shove.

"Or that I went through a five-hour surgery to save my own life, only for the doctors to tell me I'd never carry another child again?"

Shove.

"Or do you want me to tell you that I held our baby's tiny lifeless body and cried until they forced me to give her up?"

Tears streamed down my face as I shoved him again and again.

"Or how about I tell you about the night I nearly took a whole bottle of pain pills because I had nothing left to live for. Does knowing all of this make you happy? Does it make you feel part of the experience?"

All the pain from that time filled my whole being. I wanted to hate him for putting me through that.

A sob escaped my lips, and I pounded my fists on his chest.

Kir wrapped his arms around me, holding me against him. "I'm so sorry. God, I'm so sorry."

No, I wouldn't make it easy for him.

I struggled, pulling away from him. "You don't get a free pass by saying that. I needed you. I fucking needed you. On the island, you said you failed. Yes, you failed me. You fucking failed me by not being there for me when I needed you."

"I wish I could change it. I swear." He ran a hand through his hair. "You have no idea how much I regret everything. I wish I'd been a stronger man, one worthy of you."

"Even if you were too hurt to be there physically, all I needed to know was that you were alive, and it would have helped."

"Please, Jayna, forgive me. I promise to make it up to you for the rest of my life."

I took a deep breath and looked down at my left hand where the rings Kir had given me sat. "I survived without you. I had to. The old Jayna needed you too much."

"I need you too."

"I depended on you for my happiness." I looked up at him. "I won't let myself love you to the point where it destroys me a second time."

"Jayna, you are everything to me. I'll do what it takes for you to believe I won't ever let you down again."

I was too scared to believe him. But how could this work without trust?

After a few moments, I wiped the tears from my eyes and asked, "Where do we go from here?"

"You tell me. I'm at your mercy."

When I said nothing, he slowly walked up to me, stopping when he was near enough to touch me.

We stared at each other, so many emotions heavy between us.

"I want to tell you something. You are my happiness, always have been. You were the light in my dark world. I lived by the rules of the streets, doing things that could have landed me in jail or dead and you saw something worthy. Do you have any idea what it does to a man to have a woman like you love them?

"After the accident, when I woke up with God knows how many things stuck in me, I couldn't find you and the guys said they told you I died, I felt as if my world was gone. I depended on you just as much as you depended on me.

"Maybe that was the moment I broke. I don't know. I just know I couldn't dig myself out of that hole."

A hiccup escaped my lips. "I had a right to be there for you. I would have been there for you."

He stepped closer, peering down at me. "I know I fucked up.

All I ever wanted to do was to protect you, even if it was from me."

"You don't think I know what it's like to live with a monster? One fucking raised me. Nothing could be worse than that bastard."

"I couldn't risk putting you in danger."

"Being born Ashok Shah's daughter puts me in danger."

"It's not the same thing."

"Maybe not, but none of this—and I mean *none* of this—would have happened if we'd never met. I'm the one who put you in danger. It was my fault you were on Papa's radar in the first place. It makes me wish I'd never gone to the fight that night, then neither of us would have had to deal with the pain of being together."

"You fucking saved me. I'll never regret one second of being with you. In you, I found a piece of my soul."

"Then why did you leave me behind? You made all the decisions for me."

"Now the decision is all yours. You make the call on whether we have a future or not." Kir turned, dropping his head and wiping his hand over his face. "I won't force you to be with me, and if you can't forgive me, I'll have to accept it."

He moved to go inside.

What was he doing? This couldn't be the end.

Just as his foot crossed the threshold of the door, I asked with a tremor in my voice, "You'd walk away from us after all this?"

"If that was what you wanted," he answered, not turning but bracing his palms on the doorframe.

"All this, and you won't fight for us?"

"Dammit, Jayna." He dropped his head. "I am fighting for us. But if there is no hope, what chance do I have?"

"I never said we didn't have a chance. Do you think I would have agreed to any of this if there wasn't a chance?"

"This is always going to be between us. If you can't forgive me, what hope do I have?"

"You wanted me to stop holding back. You wanted me to tell you about that time. Do you have any idea how raw that feels? I'm scared. Why can't you understand that?"

He turned. "Don't you think I'm scared too? I'm fucking pretending to be another man so I can make my way back to you. I'm scared that even if you stay with me, I'm going to live my life wondering if you'll leave because you can't forgive me."

The vulnerability and resignation on his face had me wanting to reach out, but I knew he was right. I hadn't given him any indications I was going to stay in this.

I couldn't lie to myself anymore. I wouldn't have done any of this if I didn't see us together at the end. I'd used the pain of the mugging and the deception to keep Kir at a distance. There would be no other man for me.

I swallowed, feeling tears burn my throat. "I didn't want to admit it, even to myself, but I forgave you before I left the island. You know better than anyone that there isn't a person on earth who can make me do something I don't want to do."

"What are you saying?"

"We made vows to each other long ago. Even before we actually married. Through thick or thin, nothing was going to break us. Do you remember saying that to me?"

He shifted to come toward me and then stopped. "I also said you were mine. Are you mine?"

Closing my eyes for a second, I released a deep breath and then said, "I've always been yours. Even when I fought it, I never stopped being yours. We've always belonged to each other."

We stared, neither of us moving.

Then after what felt like hours, he growled, "Mine."

He stalked toward me, fisting my hair, tugging my head back, and covering my lips with his.

Immediately, goosebumps prickled my skin, and all the pent-up need from the last six weeks erupted.

God, I missed this so much.

The feel of his mouth was incredible, something I'd craved for so long. He tasted so good, so intoxicating. I clutched his shoulders, feeling his muscles flex under my fingers.

His tongue slid against mine, rolling and stroking in that wicked way that always sent shivers down my spine. I pressed myself against his hard body, needing so desperately to get closer.

We ate at each other's mouths, savoring and losing ourselves in the kiss.

Kir gripped my ass and rolled his hips so the hard length of his cock rubbed against my sensitive clit. Desire flooded my core, making me gasp and break the kiss.

"I need more," I said through a breathless whisper.

"More is definitely on the table." He glided his fingers up my spine to the zipper of my dress and then lowered it. "I want you naked."

"Yes, naked."

Stepping back, I let the dress fall from my shoulders and

then reached behind me to unfasten my bra, dropping it to the floor.

The way Kir's dark, almost onyx eyes hungrily ate up my body had my nipples pebbling and me aching to press my thighs together to relieve the need building inside my core.

Kir pulled me toward him and cupped my breast as he covered my mouth with his again.

God, I needed this man.

"Now I want you naked," I murmured.

"Be my guest. Aren't you the one who likes to undress me?"

He was right. I loved touching him.

As my fingers worked the buttons of his shirt free, I trailed kisses along his scarred jaw and neck. He shivered and then arched his throat up into the graze of my lips.

He had no idea how he affected me. His desire pushed mine. He was such a potent man, always had been.

After I pushed his shirt from his body, I went to work on his pants. But instead of sliding the material down his legs, I only lowered it enough to free his gorgeous engorged cock.

Gripping his thick, hard length, I pumped up and down. The play of desire on Kir's face sent a spasm deep inside my pussy.

A drop of precum beaded the head of his length, making my mouth water. Slowly, I lowered to my knees and licked the drop of his arousal.

"Jayna." His voice was hoarse. "Later. Right now, I want to be inside you."

"No, now." I held his gaze, smiled, and then engulfed him, taking him deep.

"Fuck, Jayna." He fisted my hair, throwing his head back.

I began an unhurried and steady rhythm, moving up and

down. I followed each stroke of my mouth with a squeeze in the same direction with my palm.

A moan escaped his lips. "Just like that. Your mouth is dangerous."

I hummed around him, loving the feel of his velvety cock sliding against my lips. His hold on my head tightened, and his hips took over the rhythm.

I gripped his firm ass, knowing that he was in charge now. He pumped in and out from between my lips. His breaths grew shallow, and I readied myself to swallow his release.

Abruptly he pulled out of my mouth, tucking himself back in his pants. "No more. I'm not coming like this."

He brought me to my feet and then ran his thumb over my swollen lips before kissing them. "I'm going to fuck you now."

"I'm…I'm okay with that," I responded, deepening the kiss.

He lifted me by my thighs, and I wrapped my arms and legs around him, squirming as the press of his thick, fabric-covered cock teased my wet pussy lips.

Kir walked us into the penthouse. "Which way to your room?"

I pointed to a hallway behind me, and he took us in that direction.

With only the lights from the hallway illuminating the room, he laid me on the bed and crawled over me, caging me with his arms. He leaned down, kissing me then moving lower. The abrasion of his stubble against my sensitive skin was an erotic torture of wanting to squirm away and pull him closer.

I felt his lips curve. He knew I was ticklish.

He stepped off the bed, removing his shoes and pushing his pants and boxers down. The dim light from the hallway set a glow around him, emphasizing the sculpted angles and muscles of his incredible body.

Lifting onto one elbow, I offered him my hand. He stared at it for a second before threading his fingers with mine. I drew him closer as he moved over me and then settled between my legs. Our mouths found each other again.

God, he tasted incredible. I'd never get enough of his kisses.

Slowly, Kir positioned the blunt head of his cock and then pushed into my sopping pussy.

"Kir," I moaned, raising my hips to meet his thrust.

He set an almost excruciatingly slow pace, with long, deep strokes designed to awaken every nerve in my body but never send me over. It was a delicious torture to drive me out of my mind with need.

"Harder, Kir. I need harder," I demanded, gripping his ass and digging my nails into the firm flesh.

He bit my lower lip, not enough to hurt but just to give it a sting. My pussy quivered around his girth in response.

"Please, I need you to stop teasing me and fuck me like you mean it."

"Is this what you need?" He pulled out to the tip and slammed in, making me gasp and arch up.

"Yes," I cried out, clenching my eyes shut. "Just like that. Don't stop."

Kir lifted onto his arms, staring down at me. "I wanted to be gentle with you. Give you the tenderness you deserve. But you seem to want the animal side of me."

I clutched at his arms, reveling in the feel of him moving inside me. "I love the animal side of you. I love all sides of you, even the ones that make me crazy."

He stopped moving, making me cry out.

"What are you doing?"

"Say it again."

"Say what?"

He lowered his head until we were nose to nose. "Say it again."

"Oh." I cupped his face and kissed him. "I love you."

He closed his eyes, taking in my words. "I was afraid you'd never say it to me again."

"I never stopped loving you. Even when I wanted to hate you, I couldn't. You are it for me, Kiran King."

"I love you, Princesa."

Tears filled my eyes, making me realize how much I needed the words too.

"Kir."

"Yes."

"I need you to fuck me now."

He turned his face into my hand, kissing my palm. "Anything for you, Mrs. King."

Kir shifted his hips and then thrust deep, setting a relentless pace. My pussy flooded with desire and spasmed.

"Yes. I'm almost there."

"I know." Kir slid his fingers between our bodies and to the sensitive nerves of my clitoris.

All it took was a graze and I detonated. "Oh God, Kir."

My back bowed and stars flashed behind my eyes as my pussy clamped down on Kir's pistoning cock. My orgasm rocketed through every cell in my body, and my mind clouded with ecstasy.

"Again," Kir said, continuing to circle and stroke the sensitive bud at the apex of my sex.

"I don't think I can."

I hadn't even come down from the first one. There was no way I could come again.

"I know you can."

I clutched at his shoulders, barely able to breathe as the need deep inside my core built again.

"That's it, baby. Let go." Kir rolled his hips, hitting the spot only he'd ever found. "I've got you."

My back bowed and I dug my nails into his arms as a cascade of overwhelming sensation washed over me.

Kir continued to pump in and out of my soaked, spasming core until his rhythm faltered and his cock swelled, forcing him to come hot and deep inside me.

21

KIRAN

I WOKE TO THE SCENT OF COFFEE IN THE AIR AND SUNLIGHT streaming onto my face. I stared at the ceiling, feeling emotionally raw yet more settled than I'd felt in the longest time.

Jayna and I would make it.

I'd bear the shame of knowing she'd thought of taking her life. She was the strongest person I'd ever met, and because of me, she'd broken.

She'd forgiven me, but I knew we still had a long road ahead of us to move past the pain I'd caused her. And if it meant she punched me or raged at me, I'd take it. I would never let her down again.

Rubbing the sleep from my eyes, I sat up and then looked over at the clock on the side table. Five forty-five.

Damn. Why the hell was she up so early? Might as well join her and find out.

Rising from the bed, I pulled on my boxers, then after a quick trip to the bathroom to freshen up, I walked into the living room to find a carafe of coffee sitting on a heating plate with a cup next to it.

Looking to my right, I found Jayna leaning over a table in the far corner of her balcony, working on the laptop, wearing something that looked like a cross between a robe and a kimono.

Jayna always loved her fashion, even when it never made sense to the rest of us.

I tilted my head and realized that her ass and pussy were completely visible with her at that angle.

Making my way to the door, I opened it and stepped out onto the terrace.

"You're naked under that thing."

She turned with a smile, leaning back on the edge of the table. "Yes, I am. Want to take advantage?"

"Out here?" I asked, stepping toward her and then caging her with a hand on either side of her.

She stared into my eyes. "Yes. I want to be with you in the sunshine."

All of a sudden, I remembered Nik saying, *"All you need to do is walk out into the sunshine."*

This woman was my sunshine.

"Aren't you worried about someone watching?"

She gestured with her chin over her shoulder. "I have someone who watches me. He sits over there in the shadows near the water."

Instead of looking in the direction she said, I continued to gaze at her. "It was the only way I could be close to you."

"I know now." Her voice grew soft as her fingers touched my jaw. "For the longest time, I thought you were a ghost haunting me, then every time I saw you, I started viewing you as my guardian angel."

I closed my eyes, dropping my forehead against hers. "I promise to make it up to you."

She cupped my face. "We have to move forward, Kir. That's the only way this is going to work."

"Is it that simple?"

"Yes, it is." She paused. "Well, marriage is never simple. However, we've been through enough shit over the years that I have no doubt we can make it past this."

"I don't deserve you, but I'm never letting you go." I threaded my fingers into her hair, drawing her toward me and sealing our lips together.

God, this woman tasted better than the finest wine.

I lifted her onto the table, closing her laptop and moving it to a nearby chair. She wrapped her arms and legs around my waist, pulling me against her slick pussy.

"Are you sure you don't want to go inside? Anyone with a telescope or a camera could see us."

A wicked smile touched her lips. "Since when have I cared about that? If I recall, there are plenty of times I put us in compromising positions."

"Yes, I remember, I corrupted the Shah princess."

Jayna reached between us, untying her robe and pulling the long silk belt free. "I could swear that it was the other way around. Before me, the enforcer of the King brothers was rarely, if ever, seen in public and never caught doing something scandalous with any woman."

Jayna's exhibitionist side had surprised the hell out of me when we'd first gotten together. There wasn't a place she wouldn't have let me fuck her. And the more the possibility of getting caught, the more it turned her on.

"True, but then again, only a fool would say no when the woman of his dreams wants him to pleasure her at one of her clubs." I set a hand on her chest, pushing her back onto the table, and let her robe open up to expose the centerline of her beautiful body.

"Then service me so anyone with a telescope or a camera is scandalized." She reached over her head, grasping the railings of the balcony. "Besides, this will play into the Silva cover, don't you think? I did start an affair with him last night."

"Or—" I lowered into a chair, draped her legs over my shoulders, and then rubbed my stubble on the inside of her thigh, "—it could be the beginning of the return of Kiran King."

"What?" She sat up, grabbing my face.

Maybe I should have waited to discuss this.

I met her gaze. "I've settled things with Hector. He's not a problem anymore. Now it's time to finish things with your father and his partners."

She shook her head and straddled my lap. "No. I will not let them target you again. Do you hear me? I can handle them."

I pushed the hair back from her face. "You wanted a life with Kir, not Antoni. This is the way. You had to know I would have to come out in public sooner or later."

"I will not let him take you from me again."

"You're not going to lose me. I won't make the same

mistakes twice. Plus, stepping out as myself adds a layer of protection for you."

"I already told you. I don't need you to protect me all the time. I have things handled."

She was not hearing me.

"It's who I am. It's what I do. For the family and especially for you." I stared into her eyes.

I braced myself for an argument, but instead, she cocked her head slightly to the side as if she was studying my face and then said, "You're serious about coming back. No more hiding."

"No more hiding."

"And you're just going to step out as Kir, no explanations? Nothing?"

"I think my face should say enough about where I went, but other than that, no. I'm a King. We make our own rules."

"And what about the fact I obtained all of your assets after your reported death?"

"They're still yours. It's not as if I had my hands in any of it before the accident."

"Fucking Kings, always full of answers," she muttered, shaking her head. "Arrogant asses, the bunch of you."

"We are who we are. Though I need to clarify something."

"What's that?"

"You'll only ever fuck this King." I gripped her hips. "Now I have a choice for you."

She narrowed her gaze. "A choice? Let me hear it."

"Fast and hard or slow and thorough?"

Her pupils dilated, turning her irises into golden rings, and her palms slid over my forearms. "Fast and hard."

Leaning down, I captured her lips.

"Kir," she moaned and then wrapped her arms around my neck.

My palms slid up her waist, along her ribs, and higher until I had her gorgeous breasts in my hands. I pulled the straining tips of her nipples, tugging and pinching, making her cry out from the pleasure and pain of it. All the while, eating at that delicious mouth of hers.

"Enough foreplay. I need you in me." Jayna pulled back and reached for the waistband of my boxers, pushing it down.

I couldn't help but laugh. "Impatient as ever."

"Kir, shut up and fuck me." She gripped the base of my cock and pumped from root to tip.

I covered her hand with mine and squeezed. Her breaths grew shallow, and a mewled whimper escaped her pouty lips.

"Now. Please." Jayna guided me to the entrance of her soaked pussy.

Sliding one arm under her robe and around her waist, I pulled her toward me, slamming balls-deep into her.

"Oh God," she cried out.

I set a hard, relentless pace, fucking her so hard the table pounded against the balcony railing.

"More," she demanded. "Yes, like that."

Her nails dug into my arms as her heels pressed into my ass while I continued to pummel her pussy.

When her orgasm shot through her, she screamed her pleasure, arching back and squeezing her eyes tight.

Her pussy walls contracted so hard around me, I felt my balls draw up, and there was no help but to follow her with my own release.

I'd barely pulled from Jayna's body and caught my breath when I saw the glint of light on the beach that looked like the lens of a camera reflecting the sunlight.

I narrowed my eyes. Was that pointed at us?

Motherfuckers.

"It looks as if the cameras have found us. Word is going to spread that you had a guest last night."

"We knew that would happen." Jayna lifted her head from my shoulder and glanced in the direction I looked. "I wonder who they will report you as? I hope Papa gets those pictures and a vein pops in his head."

"What's the point of taunting him? You're daring him to come after you. Isn't once enough?"

She gave no other outward reaction but a slight pursing of her lips. Her tell. Something that always gave away when she was holding back.

"He didn't come after me. He sent someone else to do his dirty work." She slipped from the table, grabbing the tie to her robe and wrapping it around herself. "Besides, he deserves everything he gets."

She strolled into the penthouse as if she hadn't a care in the world.

I followed her in and leaned against the doorframe. "Haven't I finally earned your secrets?"

She stopped midstep, turned, and then released a breath. "You have."

"Then tell me what you're hiding." I took a step toward her and then smiled. "Besides your mother's settlement."

Jayna's lips curved up at the corner. "Discovered that, did you?"

"Among other things. Amazing what one comes across when the Little Rabbit gets involved."

Jayna scowled. "Dani wouldn't have said a damn thing."

"True. But she does have a husband who has free rein of her gallery. Nik overheard a conversation Dani was having with Lilly at the gallery. Or should I say, it was more of a very heated ass-chewing."

"That was nearly six weeks ago. You've known this for that long and never said anything?"

"You told me I hadn't earned your secrets. I was waiting until I had to bring it up."

"I see."

I moved closer to her. "Where did you hide your mother's money?"

"It's technically not hidden."

I glared at her. "Jayna. Out with it."

"Let's just say Mummy liquidated all of her physical assets to her daughter's various companies and then transferred the profits to accounts in Switzerland."

"How the fuck did you manage this without anyone noticing?"

"Danika isn't the only smart one in the family. As much as it kills me to admit it, Ashok Shah's two children did inherit something from their fucked-up father. I despise that man, but there is no doubt he is a genius with a keen business sense. Greed is his downfall, not his ability to build an empire."

"And where do Danika and Lilly fall into this?"

"They provided their services to hide my activities from nosy-assed people until everything was officially executed."

"What are you leaving out?"

"I took all the companies Papa put under my name and placed them in a trust with the King brothers as beneficiaries if anything happens to me."

"Did you do this as payback for trying to force you into a marriage because of those companies?"

"Not for that reason."

"You told Danika that you didn't want to fight him when you moved here. That you didn't want to have anything to do with him. What changed?"

Jayna's eyes filled with pain. "I kept seeing the ghost of my dead husband, kept remembering my murdered child, kept watching my mother suffer because she stood up for herself. It made me want to make it very difficult for that bastard to ever get his happily ever after. Especially since I'd never have mine because of him."

"I can understand wanting to get back at him." I set a hand on her hip. "But you literally put a target on yourself. You wanted him to come after you. Why?"

"What did I have to lose? I was protecting the people who mattered, then letting the chips fall."

Her saying that felt as if she'd stabbed me in the heart. She'd talked about wanting to take her life when she was at her lowest, but this was on a different level. It was as if she was setting up everything so if someone killed her, there weren't any loose ends.

"When you found out I was alive, didn't you believe we had

even a slight possibility of a future? It didn't make you change your mind?"

"It did."

"Then why go through with it?"

"Because I refused to let Papa win this time. When I learned about you, I altered my plans for a different result."

"And what was that?"

"Leverage. Danika has hers against Papa to keep him in line. I needed my own."

"I'm not following. How does antagonizing him give you leverage?"

"Those companies under my name are extremely profitable, especially one with a property in Botswana with a recently discovered diamond pipe. Which means I've come into a large sum of money. Papa needs my cooperation to fund his campaign and to keep Shah International out of bankruptcy. I'm going to offer it. I'll even pay off his debt to Arun Joshi."

"In other words, you're going to put your father on an allowance. And if he steps out of line, you'll pull funding."

"Exactly. The most important things in Papa's life are his company and image. I'll give him the means to keep both pristine. All the while, he will know I'm pulling his strings. I'm the one who controls his destiny."

"Baby, I'm not sure he's going to fall in line that easily. The second he finds out what you've done, he's going to come for you."

"He already knows. That's what I was working on this morning when you came outside. A nice little email detailing my offer and forty-eight hours to accept or decline."

I shook my head and closed my eyes. I wanted to shake her

and then lock her in a bunker so no one could get to her. People like Ashok Shah weren't going to roll over and let anyone walk over them. He'd orchestrated my accident and the bus crash that killed my parents just to get rid of Sam's mom. There was nothing that man wouldn't do to get what he wanted.

"Do you have any regard for your safety?" I leaned in until I was at eye level with her.

"Stop worrying. Papa needs me too much." Jayna cupped my face. "Plus, you've got me watched nonstop. Hell, between your Solon people and Fox heading my security, I'm living in a virtual Fort Knox. Nothing is going to go wrong."

22

JAYNA

"Don't you have Antoni Silva shit to do?" I glared at Kir as he pulled into the garage of Hira around noon.

"No."

For the last few hours, Kir had reduced his vocabulary to a handful of words and growls. I couldn't understand why everyone was always okay with Danika doing all her crazy hacker shit and then acting as if I was a ticking bomb when I'd executed something similar. Hell, she'd helped me do it.

"I don't need you with me at every moment."

"Too bad."

"You're pissing me off."

"Good. Then you know how I feel."

"As I said, I have Fox. Having you breathing down my neck is fucking annoying."

"Too bad."

I clenched my teeth. "If I didn't love you, I'd punch you in the face right now."

"At least we have that."

The second he pulled into a parking space, I jumped out of the car and rushed to the employee entrance. He would need access using the fingerprint reader, and he wasn't authorized. I pressed my finger to the screen, opened the door, and closed it as Kir grabbed the handle.

I could hear Kir smack the door and scream something at me, but I ignored it.

This was getting ridiculous. He'd sat with me through my meetings at Ladai, and now he was at Hira to drive me nuts.

Even Dani's assurance that Papa wouldn't do anything to jeopardize his political aspirations hadn't calmed Kir. He kept saying something about his gut and he wasn't going to go against it.

He banged on the door again, and this time I paused. I really needed to get it into his thick skull that I could handle Papa.

Releasing a sigh, I turned around. I couldn't leave Kir sitting in the car, even if a small part of me wanted to make him stew.

Just as I neared the large metal door, a loud boom exploded around me, forcing me instinctively to crouch down and cover my ears.

Oh God.

Ignoring the ringing in my ears, I pushed myself to my feet and opened the door. Smoke filled the garage, making it impossible to see anything. My heart stopped when a large burning mass came into view where Kir's car was supposed to be. The explosion had blown all the other cars on their sides and into the walls of the garage.

"Kir!" I screamed.

No, this couldn't be happening. We'd gone through too much. I couldn't lose him again.

"Kir, please answer me, dammit." Tears filled my eyes.

Moving closer to the burning Porsche, I scanned around the area, not seeing anything. Then I focused on something in the emergency stairwell that looked like a body and everything inside me shook.

"Please, God, let it be Kir." I shifted to run in that direction, but a hand clamped over my face and a needle poked into the side of my neck, causing my mind to cloud and the world to disappear.

"WAKE UP, JAYNA."

I whimpered as a hand touched my face. My head felt as if it would explode at any second, and my stomach churned. I opened my lids and tried to focus. Everything was a haze, as if there was a film on my eyes.

"Jayna, you need to drink this. It will help."

Luke? What was he doing here? Where was Kir?

The explosion. Oh God, Kir.

I jerked up. Then, immediately fell back down when pain burst in my head. I curled into a ball.

"What did you do to me?"

"It's a side effect of the sedative. You'll start to feel better after you drink this." Luke lifted me and placed a glass to my lips. "Swallow."

He forced the liquid into my mouth, causing me to gag and then cough.

"Stop." I tried to bat his hands away, but he kept pushing the glass to my lips.

"I need you to sober up. We have things to discuss."

Knowing I had no choice, I parted my lips and drank down the disgusting fizzy liquid, trying not to throw up.

"In about twenty minutes, things will settle." Luke set me back down onto a sofa-like thing and rose. "Rest until then. Just know the more you cooperate, the faster you'll get back home."

I closed my eyes, not saying anything in response to Luke's words. All my thoughts swirled around the explosion in the garage.

Kir. *Please be okay.*

A tear spilled down my cheek. This was not the end of my story with him. I refused to believe we'd come back together just for it to end like this.

After lying in one spot for a few minutes, I felt strong enough to sit up. I breathed through the dizziness and tried to focus on the room around me. Slowly, the area came into view, and I realized I was on a boat. No, not a boat. It was a yacht.

That explained the nausea. It always took me an hour or so to acclimate to being on the water for any trip.

Pushing down the discomfort in my stomach, I scanned the large lounge where Luke had placed me.

None of this made sense. Why would Luke do this? Taking me wouldn't get him anything. Had he been playing me this whole time?

Mummy's words filled my head. *"I don't trust that family."*

I clenched my teeth. Yep, I'd let myself get played.

I wanted so desperately to have a friend who felt the same way about our childhoods that I'd ignored the signs.

All of a sudden, another bout of nausea hit me. Could Luke have orchestrated his fiancée Seema's heart condition and death? No, I wouldn't go there. I had enough to think about.

Most of all, figuring out what the hell Luke wanted with me.

"Good. You're feeling better," Luke said as he came into the lounge with three men I knew were his security team. "Let's have a chat."

"Why am I here?"

"You know why." He took the seat across from me and leaned forward. "It's time to collect on a deal made over a decade ago. No matter what you believe, there is no getting out of it, for Shah or you."

"You're out of your mind."

"I've waited. I let you get your childish rebellion out of your system. I even let you fuck other men. I'm done with that."

Let me? The fuck, he let me do anything.

"You're delusional. I make my own decisions. I'm not some commodity to sell, no matter what anyone believes."

"That's where you're wrong. As the heir to Shah International, you are a commodity. Your father used you as the collateral to expand his empire. Upon your father's death, you and, in turn, our children inherit everything."

I was a fucking idiot who should have listened to her mother. Hell, I should have listened to Kir and Danika too. Luke had played the long game, thinking I would come to my senses.

My God. I'd almost fallen for it.

"It was you. You set up the attack on me after our lunch. I thought it was Papa."

"He's too busy trying to save his campaign to focus on you at the moment. Now I want to know: how did Silva make the scene disappear?"

"What makes you think it was Silva who did anything? I am a King. I have connections that could boggle the mind."

"The King connections don't have that type of reach in Miami. You're Silva's whore, and he's very attached to you. Some would say he's in love with you."

Luke gestured, and one of his men handed him a folder. He opened it and then laid pictures one by one on the table between us.

They were images of Kir and me from the club as we danced, from our date with Kir kissing my forehead as we left the restaurant, and the last two were from last night and this morning of us on my penthouse balcony.

Kir's face was in shadows. However, anyone who saw the pictures would have no doubt of the level of intimacy we shared or how we felt about each other. It was as if the world disappeared when we were together.

I refused to believe he hadn't survived the explosion. And I refused to let this bastard break me.

I held his gaze and then said, "What's wrong with a woman whoring herself to a man who's in love with her? It has its perks."

Luke clenched his jaw. "How long have you been fucking him?"

"Years."

"At least that criminal can't plant a kid in your damaged cunt. The only way you'll ever be a mother is if another woman takes your egg and does your job for you."

Everything in me froze, and rage filled me on a level like I hadn't felt in a long time.

"How do you know this? I've only ever told two people. My mother doesn't even know."

Ignoring my question, he glared at me before he paced for a second, paused, and then moved around the table to tower over me.

"All you had to do was fall in line, like the rest of us. The hell I was going to let you bring another man's kid into the world."

All the breath left my lungs, and then my body trembled.

I wasn't sure what possessed me. I launched myself at Luke, kneeing him in the stomach and then punching him in the face. "You killed my little girl. You fucking monster."

Luke fell to the ground, and I jumped on him and continued to whale on him until someone pulled me off him.

"I will kill you, and you will be as dead as my baby. Do you hear me?" I thrashed against the hold on me. "I hate you. I hate you."

Luke stood and grabbed me by the throat, squeezing so hard, I could barely breathe. Rage filled his eyes as blood dripped from his nose and the corner of his mouth.

"You've only seen the nice side of me, Jayna. Pushing me too far will result in dire consequences."

"Just know, if you kill me, the Kings get everything. I've made sure of it."

"Not if you marry me." His hold on my neck tightened.

"L-like hell I will," I gasped.

Luke released me, and I couldn't help but inhale deep and sag against the giant holding me.

Luke walked over to a bar, grabbed a napkin, and wiped the blood from his face before he poured himself a drink and tossed it back, swallowing all of it in one go.

"You will. You are going to fulfill the deal made with your father. He owes my family and so do you. He isn't going to get out of anything by offering to write us a check for his debt to us. It doesn't work that way."

This meant Papa had accepted the terms of the deal I sent him. That was the only way he could pay off Luke's family or any other investor.

Fucking great time to find out.

"I will not marry you. Papa tried to force me when I was a teenager and you saw how well that went. Just try me now."

"Are you so sure you're willing to risk your mother's life? Or what about your bitch cousin, Danika? Don't think I won't use those you love to get what I want."

"Do you really think they aren't protected?"

"You mean like your boyfriend, Silva? Nothing is foolproof. If I got to him with all of his security, I could get to your mother and Danika."

"Touch a hair on Dani's head, and Nik will use everything in his empire to kill you."

"It's your head you need to worry about. You know there is no choice, Jayna. You have to marry me."

"No."

Luke stalked toward me, hauling me toward him. "In a few minutes, an officiant will arrive and you will marry me. Do you understand?"

"Not happening," I bit out. "Find someone else to fulfill your purposes."

"Do you actually believe I want to fuck another man's whore? All I need is your signature and your eggs." The sound of boats approaching reverberated around the yacht. "And here he is."

"Even if you force me to marry you, it wouldn't be legal."

"Why is that?"

Before I could answer, guns cocked from behind me, and someone said, "Because she's already married."

Relief and fear warred inside me, hearing Kir's voice. I wanted to turn to see if he was hurt, but I knew I had to stay calm.

"You're dead." Luke's voice shook as his grip on my arm tightened to an almost excruciating level. "Shah and my father made sure of it."

"They apparently weren't thorough with their job. Though I did come back with a few souvenirs from the experience."

Before I knew what was happening, Luke jerked me toward him and had me in a headlock against him with a gun pointed at my head.

I clawed at his arm but reined in the split second of panic and held onto his shirt.

"Let her go, Joshi. You can't win this."

"She's going to stay right here."

The hell I was. I had backup now. I was far from helpless. Plus, Luke's attention was on Kir and the team with him.

Taking a deep breath, I released my grip on Luke's arm and then let my feet fall out from under me, catching Luke off guard and causing him to release his hold on my neck. Immediately I crouched down, pivoted, and kicked the backs of his knees with everything I had, forcing him to fall forward.

Before I could make another move, a swarm of people rushed into the room. Some were dressed in regular street clothes, and others were in black military fatigues. They grabbed Luke and his men, dragging them out of the lounge.

"Princesa." Kir rushed to me, pulling me against him.

Trying to catch my breath, I turned my face into his chest. "You brought Solon to get me?"

"And others."

"You're okay. I was so scared. The car."

"I was about to climb the stairwell to the main entrance when the bomb went off. It knocked me out for a few seconds." He kissed the top of my head and then helped me to stand. "Those were some impressive moves."

"All that training with Dillon finally came in handy."

"You mean in addition to knocking your husband on his ass?"

"Yes." I smiled. "In addition to that."

A female Solon agent dressed in black with a matching mask strolled up to us and then spoke to Kir. "You're needed outside. It's time to finish this. We have to be out of here in fifteen."

We followed behind her. I came to an abrupt stop as I stepped onto the deck when I saw the man standing in front of Luke and his men. The man looked so much like Kir that they could have been brothers, from build to the way they stood. The only differences between the two men were their skin tones and eye colors.

"Why is Hector Estefan here? I thought you made peace with him."

"I did. This is part of our agreement."

"I think we need to reevaluate our 'not discussing what happens in our businesses' thing."

"I completely agree."

"Now explain to me what he's doing here."

"I am what you would call—" Hector approached us, "—your guardian angel."

Okay, that explained nothing.

I glared at Kir.

"Let me clarify. Your husband secured my claim on my birthright and therefore, as the head of Silva Familia, I have to make sure my relatives are protected. Joshi threatened the family. We can't have that."

"In other words, it's favors."

Kir responded, "Yes. No more Antoni Silva. There is only Kiran King."

"Okay. I'm good with this."

At that moment, a noise came from the direction where Hector's men held Luke.

"Let's take care of business," Kir said, keeping me by his side. "I have a few questions for Mr. Joshi."

"No questions." Hector stepped forward. "We are in what we agreed is my territory. That means I make the rules. We're handling it *Abuelo*'s way. No civilized King shit that takes too long."

The next thing we knew, Hector drew his pistol from the back of the waistband of his pants, walked up to Luke, pointed the barrel at his head, and pulled the trigger. He continued to shoot each of the captured men.

"This *pendejo* and his people took your wife, killed your

child, and tried to kill you. In my book, this is considered mercy."

I stood there in shock. Hector was fucking insane. Well, then again, he was a mobster.

Hector turned to Kir. "Our deal will stand as long as you continue to hold up all parts we discussed."

"Understood."

"Now get lost. It's time for those of us with the stomach for it to clean up the mess."

"As I said, why get our hands dirty when a favor in the right place can buy us an army?"

Hector's attention moved to me, and he examined me as if I was some oddity. "All of this for a woman?"

"The right woman makes it worth it," Kir responded.

Hector nodded. "If you say so."

23

KIRAN

A LITTLE BEFORE SIX, MY DRIVER PULLED UP TO THE FRONT OF what was Jayna's former art gallery. It had been three days since the explosion and Jayna's kidnapping.

As with her first abduction, there was no evidence of the incident. Well, there was no way to conceal the explosion at her club. Instead, after I called in some favors, an investigation deemed the event a result of an undetected gas leak caused by construction in the area.

"Mrs. King is inside," Fox said. "Just arrived with the other Mrs. King."

I took a deep breath and readied myself to do something I hadn't done in nearly three years. Go out into public as Kiran King.

Tonight, everyone would know the Kings had secrets like them. We just held ours closer to our chests than they did.

I opened my door and stepped out into the busy streets of New York City. Looking around, I took in the area. People glanced in my direction and then went about their business, not caring as other New Yorkers lived their lives.

As I straightened my suit jacket, I felt a weight I hadn't realized sat so heavy on my shoulders lift. There was no more worrying about anyone seeing me. There was no more hiding.

I moved to the entrance and stepped through the glass doors of the gallery.

Damn, this place was incredible. The changes Danika had made engulfed the senses.

The exhibit taking center stage in the main showroom was all about birds, real and mystical. Paintings with vibrant splashes of color filled the walls, giant sculptures in bright hues hung from the ceiling, and high-dollar masterpieces were strategically placed along every walking path to catch the best light.

There was no doubt this was Danika's calling.

As I moved in closer, I found Jayna studying different sculptures.

God, she was the sexiest woman I'd ever known.

She wore a long burgundy gown with long sleeves, and her gorgeous black hair was in some artsy messy bun thing that made me want to walk up to her and make it even messier.

She shifted to the side, and I couldn't help but frown as her back came into view. I could see down to the upper curve of her ass. The only thing not exposing everything was the crazy way she had her jewelry hanging to keep her body from looking indecent.

Damn woman and her crazy fashion.

I moved in closer, leaned against a pillar near the exhibit, and waited for her to notice me.

Her fingers trailed over the edge of an enormous glass phoenix with wings of blue, red, and gold. The creature stood regal atop a pedestal of flames.

The name of the piece was *Fiery Second Chances*.

"Kir," she whispered.

"Are you saying I look like a bird?"

She whirled around and stared at me. Then her gaze took me in from head to shoes and back again.

She licked her lips and smiled. "Well, you are wearing a tux, and you have referred to them as penguin suits."

"That's true." I moved toward her. "You ready to be seen in public with me?"

She cupped my face with both of her hands and drew me to her. "Always."

I closed my eyes as she brushed her lips against mine. I knew I didn't deserve this woman. I was just thankful we'd gotten a second chance.

When she drew back, she grinned up at me and said, "Let's go put the fear of God in Daddy Dearest."

"Yes, ma'am." I offered her my arm.

She slipped hers into the crook of my elbow, and we made our way out of the gallery.

"Do you miss it?" I asked as we stepped into the car and the door closed.

"No. The gallery was Dani's from the beginning. I only went

into the art business to help her and to piss off Papa. I could never have created an exhibit like the one we just experienced. I'm not as refined as my baby cousin."

"I'd beg to differ. You are class at its finest." I threaded my fingers with hers.

"Maybe." She shifted our hands and set them between my legs, immediately causing my cock to react. "Although, I think I'm more about sweat, grit, violence, and the aura of sex."

"Is that right? You must hang out with some bad influences."

I closed my eyes and dropped my head back as she stroked me through my pants.

"I think I'm the one who's the bad influence. Who gets who to do scandalous things?" She squeezed the head of my erection, and I clenched my teeth.

"Jayna, I need you to stop, or I'm going fuck you, and I won't care who can see into the car."

"There you have it." She laughed, moving her hand into her lap. "I'm the bad influence."

"Once we finish this with your father, I plan to fuck you on every surface of the penthouse. You're not going to be able to walk when we have to go back to Miami."

"I'm okay with that."

The car pulled to a stop in front of the Andhi New York City.

Jayna reached for her clutch and offered me her hand. "Let's make your debut back into society, Mr. Kiran King."

JAYNA

. . .

I gazed up at the beautiful exterior of the hotel I'd walked through countless times during my childhood and teen years. Designed to mix the classic architecture of a French chateau with the elegant palaces of India, it made a visitor feel as if they were about to escape into a world of indulgence.

And it was true, guests of the establishment experienced the best of everything. From top-notch and friendly staff and a world-class spa to restaurants that made the biggest food snob beg for recipes.

The people who saw the darker side of the place were trained from a young age to keep quiet and do as they were told or suffer the consequences.

I swallowed, hating the way I always feared walking into the place.

"Baby, it's going to be okay. We only have to stay long enough to deliver our message. Then we can leave." Kir set a hand on my waist.

"I'm fine. It's just a damn building. It has no power over me. The one who holds all the blame is the fucking man who did it to me." I moved toward the lobby. "Let's go."

The second Kir and I stepped into the entryway, I was greeted by staff who recognized me—many of them who'd worked for the property for a decade or more.

I walked up to a painting of Papa, Mummy, and me when I was around eleven years old.

Papa wore his customary three-piece suit. Mummy had on a beautifully embroidered sari with a collection of bangles that went halfway up her forearms. She'd worn them that way to cover the bruises on her arms. And I sat next to her, clutching her hand in my designer frilly dress. I'd been so scared to move the whole time we'd sat for the portrait.

Why the fuck would he keep this up?

I clenched my teeth. The bastard wanted to make the world think he was a family man.

"This place is beautiful," Kir said, shifting my attention to him. "It has always amazed me how incredible it looks inside."

"It is. Too bad the owner is a piece of shit."

"Ashok Shah isn't the owner. He's a squatter. The owners of Shah International are you, Danika, and Sam. It was in your grandmother's will."

"No, the will says the first grandchild gets the company. Dani and I are shareholders, but the company belongs to Sam."

"He doesn't want it."

"One day, he will change his mind."

"Baby, it's not going to happen. He's as stubborn as you and Dani are."

I turned to Kir, setting a hand on his chest. "As you like to say, your gut tells you things. Well, my gut says Sam is going to take every damn thing owed to him and more."

"And when that happens, you and Dani will be by his side," Kir added.

"Exactly. Everyone thinks Nik is the dangerous one. Sam is the powder keg no one knew existed."

"For our sakes, I hope you're wrong." Kir looked at his watch. "We need to head in. Lilly and Rey are waiting for us. If we need to worry about a powder keg, it's them."

"True. Lilly isn't the sweet and nerdy girl she projects."

We made our way into the ballroom, and immediately it felt

as if all eyes were upon us. Kir seemed to stiffen next to me, and the hand he had on my lower back pressed into my skin as if he needed something to ground him.

"I'm okay." Kir looked down at me. "Why don't you introduce me to my father-in-law."

Papa stood with a group of people smiling and laughing. There was no denying he was a good-looking man for his age. He had a mix of salt-and-pepper hair and a full white beard. He dressed well and took care of his body. His public image was polished and charming, something that drew people like flies to honey.

Next to him was his fiancée, Amisha Noor, a fellow divorcée from the Indo-American community who was ten years his junior. She knew the game and played it well. She would make Papa the perfect society wife.

Lilly and Rey stepped in next to me as we moved closer to Papa and his group.

Damn, Lilly and Rey made a striking couple. Well, if they weren't always fighting. Both of them looked like models who should walk the runways of fashion week instead of spending time behind computers and doing recon work.

"You look pretty good," Rey said to Kir, smacking him on the back, and then added, "For a formerly dead man."

"Shut up, asshole. Give me the tablet."

Lilly handed Kir a pocket-sized device. "I have it set to open to the necessary documents. All he needs to do is sign."

"Thank you, Lil. You're the best." I squeezed her hand.

"Now that your work is done, let's get you back to your cave, or your father will put a hit on me." Rey offered Lilly his arm.

"Kir is right. You are an asshole."

"Probably. That doesn't change the fact I'm your keeper."

Instead of staying with them to hear the rest of whatever they were talking about, I pulled Kir with me toward Papa.

"Couldn't we have stayed a little longer? It was getting interesting. I've never known Rey to antagonize anyone like he does Lilly."

I opened my mouth to respond to Kir's remark but stopped when I noticed Papa's look in our direction when someone pointed to us.

Surprise flashed on his face, and then his eyes narrowed.

"Get ready." Kir wrapped an arm around my waist and drew me closer to his side.

As Papa made his way toward us, he paused for a brief second, looking at Kir, and then continued in our direction.

"You're not dead."

"Doesn't look that way."

"I see."

Something flashed in his gaze, and then a calculating grin touched his lips. "Tell me, Jayna, does your husband know you've been whoring yourself to Antoni Silva?"

I expected nothing less than a cutting remark from him. He'd called me worse.

"Yes, he knows," Kir answered and then leaned forward so only Papa and I could hear. "And her husband is fine with her whoring herself to him."

"Why are you here?"

"To remind you everyone has to eventually pay the piper for their sins."

"You think to threaten me?"

"It's not a threat. It's a fact. You should ask your friend Lukesh Joshi. He paid well for his debts."

"Where is he?"

"Somewhere between here and Puerto Rico. Luke owed me a debt, and the Kings always collect."

A tremor shook Papa's hand. "What did you do to him?"

"Absolutely nothing. If anything happened to him, it wasn't by my hands."

"I don't believe you."

"Does it look as if I care?" Kir stared at Papa, letting the rage he wanted to unleash on him show. "There are consequences for our choices. You chose to get rid of me. I can get over that. Do you want to know what I'll never get over? The fact you assisted in the murder of my child and the near-death of my wife."

"There is no proof I'm involved in anything."

"It doesn't change the truth. Just like it doesn't change your involvement in my crash."

"So be it." There was a smugness to his words. "If this family reunion is over, I have a party to return to."

"One last thing," I said before Papa could turn.

Papa waited.

"You are now in debt to the Kings."

"How is that?"

"I'm a King. I became one the night you came to my apartment, beat me, and told me I was no daughter of yours, or did you forget?" I threaded my fingers with Kir's. "You need me to make your world continue to spin. That was the agreement you accepted. Now it's time to make it official."

"And how do you propose to make it official?"

Kir pulled out the tablet, turned it on, and handed him the stylus.

"This is your contract, detailing everything. Sign in every spot indicated, and the funds you need will arrive in the designated accounts." I touched the screen. "You shouldn't worry. I'm not going to force you to marry someone for the business or anything. Or send someone to stab you or orchestrate the murder of someone you love. I'm just going to make you depend on me for your pretty new life."

Papa took the stylus from Kir.

When he finished signing on the tablet, Papa looked at Kir. "You're about to become a laughingstock, King. Antoni Silva's fucked her all over Miami. The pictures will hit the tabloids any day."

"I have no problem with anyone knowing she fucked Antoni Silva." Kir leaned in until he was near Papa's ear. "You see, before Arin King adopted my brothers and me, we all had different names. Mine was Kiran Antoni Silva."

Realization passed over his face. "You're Victor Silva's grandson?"

Kir shifted back and, with a smirk, said, "I'm a King."

Just as Kir turned us to leave, I paused. "I hope you realize there is no Shah legacy left. Your daughter is a King, your niece is a King. Hell, your son is one. You destroyed your own family.

"Enjoy your life, but stay out of ours. If anything happens to me or mine again, I won't need the King empire to destroy you. I have the means to take apart what you love piece by piece."

With those words, I walked out of the ballroom with Kir.

The second we stepped outside the hotel into the cool New

York streets, I gasped in a breath as tears filled my eyes. "He can't hurt me anymore, Kir. But I can destroy him."

"You did good, Princesa." Kir wrapped me in his arms and held me tight. "I'm not sure whether to be scared of you or in awe."

"Afraid I'll take your job?"

He laughed into my hair. "Most definitely."

"Now, what do we do?"

"You tell me."

"You work here with your brothers."

"I can do my job anywhere. That's why they invented planes. And I've already been doing it behind the scenes."

"You'd stay in Miami for me?"

"I go where you go."

"Well then, I want to come back here. I love being around Mummy and the Miami family, but it's not home. I miss my life here."

"Then here it is." Our car pulled up. "Ready to go home?"

A thought crossed my mind, and I smiled. "Umm, are you up for some bad influencing?"

"Always." Kir's lips quirked up. "What do you have in mind?"

I grabbed the lapels of his tuxedo and stood on tiptoes until we were eye level. "There is this underground club where I met this guy. I think he was the owner. Well, we had dirty, hot sex during a fight night in one of the locker rooms, and everyone knew it. I want to reenact it."

"I know of an underground club open tonight." Kir threaded his fingers into my hair, loosening my bun. "But there is one problem."

"What is that?"

"The guy doesn't own the club anymore. His wife does. We'd have to get her permission."

"I think we can arrange that."

Are you ready to see Lilly put Rey in his place - Get the next book in the series – Deceptive Knight

Or

Start at the very beginning with Danika and Nik's unconventional love story - Dangerous King

However,

If you want something completely different, head to Vegas with – *Master of Sin*

https://geni.us/DeceptiveKnight

I am a liar, a deceiver, a devil in the dark.
I will hunt you, steal your secrets, and use them against you.
You will never see me coming.
Then I met my match.
She cut out my heart, left me bleeding, without a backward glance.
But, she's made one mistake…she stepped back to my world trying to run from her past.
She's mine, and she will soon learn there is no escape when fate says she belongs to me.

https://geni.us/dangerousking

I'm the one she should have stayed away from.
The thief, the hustler, the boy without a past or a future. A kid forged by the rules of the streets.
She sees into my darkest depths and doesn't blink an eye. She's my dream, my peace from a place I can never escape.
Then one day, she's gone, whisked into a world I refuse to taint with my touch.
Fifteen years later, she's back in my life, needing a favor only I can provide.
The street rat she once knew is now king of an empire, where every favor comes at a price.
A price, she says she is more than willing to pay. But the cost is all of her...body, mind, and soul.

https://geni.us/MasterOfSin

It was always him...
The one I shouldn't want, shouldn't crave, the one who could destroy my carefully built life.
Hagen Lykaios was the essence of sin, indulgence, and danger - everything I knew to avoid.
All it took was one unexpected touch, and he consumed me, left me begging, needy, and hungry for more.
He said if I entered his world he would corrupt me, own me, and change all that I had ever known...and you know what? *I went anyway.*

THE END

BOOKS BY SIENNA

Rules of Engagement
Rule Breaker

Rule Master

Rule Changer

Politics of Love
Celebrity

Senator

Commander

Gods of Vegas
Master of Sin

Master of Games

Master of Revenge

Master of Secrets

Master of Control

Master of Fortune

Sweetest Sin

Intrigued By Love

Street Kings
Dangerous King

Vicious Prince

Deceptive Knight

Ruthless Heir (Feb 2023)

Collections

Reckless Rome (A Cocky Hero Club Novel)

Take Me To Bed (Limited Run Anthology - 2019)

Meet Me Under The Mistletoe (Limited Run Anthology - 2021)

Nightingale (A charity anthology in support of Ukraine) - (April 2022)

Darkly Ever After (An Organized Crime Anthology) (May 2022)

ABOUT THE AUTHOR

Inspired by her years working in corporate America, Sienna loves to serve up stories woven around confident and successful women who know what they want and how to get it, both in – and out – of the bedroom.

Her heroines are fresh, well-educated, and often find love and romance through atypical circumstances. Sienna treats her readers to enticing slices of hot romance infused with empowerment and indulgent satisfaction.

Sienna loves the life of travel and adventure. She plans to visit even the farthest corners of the world and delight in experiencing the variety of cultures along the way. When she isn't writing or traveling, Sienna is working on her "happily ever after" with her husband and children.

Sign up for her newsletter to be notified of releases, book sales, events and so much more.
https://www.siennasnow.com/newsletter
contact@siennasnow.com

facebook.com/authorsiennasnow
twitter.com/sienna_snow
instagram.com/bysiennasnow
tiktok.com/@authorsiennasnow

Made in the USA
Middletown, DE
01 April 2023

27574059R00156